Praise for Alain Elkann's Pound's Silence

"Alain Elkann delineates the introverted ways of those who have made writing a profession. Or perhaps it is already art. It depends on the eyes and heart of those who look at those words, that each is a distillation of ourselves. Ezra Pound remains divisive and stinging."

Carlo Baroni, *Corriere della Sera*

"And with the same bitterness the abysmal question remains there, laden with torment and topicality: can one separate a person from his work? Can one condemn an artist and absolve the fruit of his or her ingenuity? At the bottom of this unexpected, sibylline and restless meta-novel, the answers — as they should be — must be found by the reader."

Paolo di Paolo, *la Repubblica*

"The story ends with a clever surprise by the would-be biographer. Rightly, we are used to separating political orientation and artistic production. This applies, however, to literary criticism. Nonetheless, in the creative space of a novel Elkann allows himself the freedom that those who work with the imagination can afford. And so, he inflicts on Pound an exemplary punishment for his anti-Semitism, for his compromise with Nazism and fascism. A punishment that we certainly do not reveal what it is."

Mirella Serri, *tuttolibri, la Stampa*

"A journey around the figure of one of the twentieth century's most original and visionary figures: a solidly, classically trained avant-gardist, economist, translator of Confucius, friend, editor and advisor to Yeats, Joyce, Eliot, Hemingway. But also, anti-Semite and political agitator imprisoned from 1945 to 1958 in the criminal section of St. Elizabeths Hospital in Washington on charges of treason. Is it possible to understand and reconcile these contradictory souls?"

Antonella Rea, *CronacaQui*

CROSSINGS 45

POUND'S SILENCE

for Osanna

POUND'S SILENCE

A novel

Alain Elkann

Translation by
Alastair McEwen

BORDIGHERA PRESS

Library of Congress Control Number: 2025937721

Originally published in 2024 by Bompiani.

Printed in the United States.

Published by
BORDIGHERA PRESS
John D. Calandra Italian American Institute
25 West 43rd Street, 17th Floor
New York, NY 10036

CROSSINGS 45
ISBN 978-1-59954-236-2

TABLE OF CONTENTS

PUBLISHER'S NOTE

We are delighted to be able to offer to our English-speaking readership yet another of Alain Elkann's Italian novels.

Elkann's latest novel in English, Pound's Silence, *is what seems to be a straight-forward narrative that tells the story of one person's desire – the aspiring biographer of Pound, Morli – to grasp the deepest meaning of the existence of the protagonist of modernism and imagism.*

Buona lettura!

POUND'S SILENCE

L ondon was deserted. Everything was closed, and anyone who left their home disinfected themselves and wore a protective mask.

The world had stopped, and people communicated only through smartphones, tablets, or computers. You breathed in an atmosphere of fear, suspicion, and mistrust.

Morli remained in London with Aloisia, locked in his apartment. His daughter called him and asked him to leave, but he couldn't. The only distraction was going to the supermarket to do the shopping.

At home he watched TV series, read, and cooked. He cooked roast chicken, minestrone, spaghetti with tomato and basil.

He spoke on the phone with friends and confided in them. At last he went outside with Aloisia: small, petite, she had very expressive dark blue eyes and dark brown hair that she kept loose or tied up, depending on the moment. Morli liked it when she washed her hair and left it wet, highlighting her very particular face. She could be smiling or gloomy over something that suddenly bothered or irritated her; but it was a passing cloud, because she couldn't stand being in a bad mood. She was sensual and childish and loved love. Morli had immediately fallen for her, but she had rejected him. She was still in love with another man, even though they had broken up. Aloisia agreed to be courted, but no more than that. Morli had tried and tried again until, after a year, they had made love one Sunday afternoon; after that they had never been apart.

The situation in London had become too oppressive, and they decided to go to Italy and rent a house in the countryside, on the border between Lazio and Tuscany. Months passed there in which the days went by to the rhythm of housework and walks to the dunes that led to the beach, because going to the beach itself was forbidden. In the evening the news or talk shows gave discouraging reports. Winter was slowly coming to an end, and the first shoots were appearing, then the tender little leaves, the fields were turning green and then yellow with rapeseed and red with poppies and spring was breaking out, approaching summer. Nature was exploding, birds of every kind chirping and warbling, and the wild rabbits seemed to be multiplying like never before. It was the first time that he and Aloisia had lived immersed in nature, without the noise of cars or aeroplanes. The whole world stood still.

Morli and Aloisia saw no one; they disinfected everything. Aloisia had a lot to do on the phone with her family to keep everyone close even though they were spread out all over. Morli had started to think about a book he had written years before about a famous Anglo-German painter, grandson of a great Austrian philosopher, doctor, and thinker. In the book he had wondered who that man really was, a man who had dedicated his whole life to painting and posing as a player, a seducer, with a controversial private life. Morli had been fascinated by the man who, continuing to speak English with a German accent, by delving deep and going against the flow in his work as a painter, had managed to become one of the most highly regarded artists of his time. Morli wondered whether he was a genius or not, and the doubt still lingered. He knew one of his daughters well, Billy, whom he had met in Rome when they were young. There was something disturbing and sweet in Billy's gaze and posture. Not very tall, thin, she had dark eyes and long black hair. Morli and Billy had met at various times in their lives, but they had never spoken much, and one couldn't say that they were really friends. They were friends of friends.

While Morli was in the country, he had written an email to Billy, asking what it meant to her to be the granddaughter and daughter of two geniuses. Billy had replied, "It's a privilege, but I have the right to live my own life and be myself. I adored my father because we were always joking, I was interested in his work, I didn't wonder whether he was a genius or not. He was my father; he was an artist."

Morli did not know why he had taken Billy as a point of reference for his obsession with genius. The truth was that since childhood he had nurtured a passion for the characters who had influenced history, who had become famous for having invented or done special things and for being defined as geniuses. He wanted to be a genius, a household name, but he knew it was an absurd wish because you don't become a genius.

The first wave of the pandemic had ended with the summer, and life seemed to go back to normal, but soon a second more violent wave had arrived, and Morli had gone back to be in London, and he hadn't budged from there. Aloisia stayed on in Italy.

By chance Morli had begun to take an interest in a person who according to various influential people had been a genius—a man who from a very young age had been a rebel, a mentor, a talent scout, and had a great talent himself. But before going any further with this story it is necessary to explain who Morli was.

Morli's name came about because an old lady had given him the nickname when he was a five-year-old child living with a Swiss-German governess in Turin at the Pensione Europa in Piazza Castello. Morli had been his name ever since, and when they asked him, "What kind of name is that?" he would answer, "I don't know, I was too young, but I've grown to like my non-existent name that's become mine."

Morli remembered that the old lady was called Carla Cirio, and the governess was called Mademoiselle Rolande. Morli was at the Pensione Europa because his parents were getting a divorce; he didn't know where they were or why they had left him alone with Mademoiselle Rolande. When he asked her where his parents were, she would answer vaguely, "Traveling."

Of his life as a child Morli remembered just a few disjointed things: for example, his father's convertible, a blue Oldsmobile; he remembered the beach at Deauville in Normandy and Isabelle, an Iranian girl. On the beach he had caressed Isabelle's belly and gotten his first erection. He remembered that his grandfather Vic, his mother's father, listened to classical music on a Grundig gramophone and sometimes got emotional. At the Europa guesthouse, along with Mrs. Cirio, he remembered a blonde lady with long hair, a painter from Casale Monferrato, Licia Cavalli, who had painted his portrait. Then there were the Pavia brothers who came from Egypt and studied in Turin. They were older than him and played with him.

After the Europa pensione, when his mother returned to Turin, Morli went to live with her in an apartment and dreamed of becoming a famous person when he grew up, but he didn't know how he would do that. He dreamed of different lives in which he would be the hero. Dreaming was like writing with chalk on a blackboard: You write and erase, just like when you have a dream and then it vanishes.

As the years went by, Morli met different people: on the road, in the city, in a hotel, in a restaurant. The people he had spoken to most often and most intimately were taxi drivers because, while they drove, he'd sit in the back and could only see their backs, and with them, for a moment, he said whatever came into his mind. He had always liked to talk about intimate things with strangers he would never meet again. It was like putting a message in a bottle and throwing it into the sea.

Morli lived in London and almost always ate in restaurants. He carried with him well-sharpened pencils, an eraser, a pen knife, and one or two fountain pens. He preferred piston-fillers and often traveled with a small bottle of blue or black ink in the old briefcase he had inherited from his father and that contained his essentials: keys, notebooks, medical reports, passport, medicines, a chestnut, two pairs of glasses. He was very fond of a Bloody Mary, but he rarely drank one. He loved walking in the parks of London, where there were flowers, ponds, geese, swans, lawns, and ancient trees. In the park he felt good, he felt free; a free man on a free island where he was a foreigner. He was a foreigner because his mother tongue was not English; he had not been born in

England, and those who are not English will never become English. Morli was used to being out of place because he had never had a place.

Toward the age of fifty he had decided to settle there. He appreciated the good manners and hypocrisy of the English, their passion for gossip in the popular newspapers and the defence of their privacy, their habits and traditions. He did not share the English love of the countryside, flowers, dogs, horses, and hunting. He preferred to stay in the city, had few friends, and made no effort to enter any kind of society or group. The common thread in his life, apart from his children, who were now grown up and married and had children of their own, had been women. Through them he discovered the world, and each had given him her world, her story. It is women who make the fabric of life and society, and women had ferried him from one city to another, from one experience to another. He had held many different jobs over the years. He had written novels, essays, and articles, and taught at various universities. He had worked for various publishing houses, hosted radio programs and, since retirement, had decided to write a book that might sum up his experiences. This is why he had become interested in Pound's *Cantos*, a poetic work that could be read as philosophy or autobiography. But isn't an artist's work always autobiographical?

When the pandemic broke out in London, Morli was scared, so he and Aloisia took refuge in Italy for a few months. There he had a lot of time to think about his life, his experiences, his children, and his grandchildren. The recurring thought was the regret, or rather the awareness, of not being a genius. This had tormented him for years; he wondered if it was because he hadn't worked hard enough or hadn't believed enough in himself. His regret at not being a genius was linked to two different, but equally significant, aspects. The first was that, having chosen to be a writer, he knew that his work wasn't up to his ambition, even though his books had been published and translated into various languages. Another aspect was vanity. If his work did not reach the level he desired, he couldn't be sure it would outlive him.

What Morli understood was that there are no rules to being a genius.

He decided to talk about it with Luke, the oldest of his friends who, being a philosopher and an architecture critic, understood the architecture of a human being better than anyone.

Morli had received a message from the daughter of a childhood friend of his who had died of a heart attack several years earlier after a long and tormented life. The girl wanted to meet him because she was looking for people who had known her father to talk about him and try to get to know him through their memories and their words, given that she had been six years old when he died. Morli had told her about some episodes of their youth and given her the names of people who had known him well at different periods in his life.

He had enjoyed talking about his friend and retracing the trips and moments he had lived through with him. As life slowly went on, loved ones passed away and others came along. Since his time at the Europa guesthouse as a child, Morli had become rootless, and at certain times he suffered terribly from feelings of abandonment.

He had three friends whom he spoke to almost every day: Luke, Pietro, an artist who was a childhood friend, and Fred, a poet who lived in New York.

Luke, ninety-five years old and of Polish origin, lived in an apartment full of books in Hampstead, and while working on his new book in which he described the city as a human body he would listen to classical music.

Pietro was from Turin and had lived for many years in Athens, where he painted and listened to Greek music on the radio.

Fred had lived in the same apartment on New York's Upper West Side for about fifty years and moved around as little as possible. He wrote poems, went to eat at a Greek restaurant downstairs or, every now and then, went to the Cafe Luxembourg, where he met with a friend and chatted with the waitresses when he was alone. Fred always dressed with great elegance: He had a passion for English tailors and Italian motorcycles.

During that period, Morli at times would suddenly feel anxious and call one of his friends; if they didn't answer, he would worry. Had something happened? Had they fallen ill? Only when they answered did he feel relieved. It was the year of the voice: hearing each other's voices. Knowing that you are alive.

Morli and Pietro talked about intimate things; they confided in each other and consoled each other about their loves and their jobs. Their shared childhood in Turin had been a strong point of reference for them, even though they had left that city many years before.

His relationship with Luke was one that had been created over time, especially since Morli had gone to live in London and since Mary, Luke's wife, had died. Morli had felt the need to protect his friend.

Before the pandemic, they'd been in the habit of having dinner together in a seafood restaurant near the Wallace Collection or in Luke's club on Brook Street. Luke always ordered the same things: fish, white wine, and a dessert. They talked for hours about friends, books, memories, and above all about a mutual friend, an Italian writer who sent his books to both of them with a dedication. They knew he was a man of vast culture and intelligence, but they weren't sure he was a great writer.

Morli was interested in Luke's relationship with Judaism and his conversion to Catholicism. Luke was a Polish Jew who had emigrated from Warsaw to London shortly before the war broke out. He spoke Yiddish and had converted to Catholicism after meeting the French philosopher Gabriel Marcel. Luke had become a devout and observant Catholic, which annoyed Mary, who was Jewish like him and had converted to Catholicism during the war to escape racial persecution but was not a believer. The question of religion remained a slippery subject between Morli and Luke.

Fred was an American poet from St. Louis who had fallen in love with New York and could not conceive of living anywhere else. His favorite poets included Eliot, Pound, and Montale, but he didn't talk about them much. He had written a few screenplays but had soon given that up to be just a poet. Since he stopped drinking and smoking one unfiltered Camel after another, he spent his days writing and talking on the phone. Morli and Fred talked about everything from health to politics and mutual friends. At the end of their long phone conversations Fred would always say to him, "You have to come and live in New York. What are you doing in London? You belong here." Fred was proud to be an American and to have studied at Harvard, where he had established the foundations of his transcontinental English.

Pietro's watercolors were like poems, and Morli envied his friend for his being a poet. Poets fascinated him because they have always existed, and poetry is a necessity of human life.

This was one of the reasons why Morli had begun to take an interest in Ezra Pound, a poet whose destiny was complex. His life had been a blend of love, intolerance, and hatred for the mediocrity of his country, the United States. It was for this reason, he had chosen while still young the life of an expatriate—first in Venice and then in London, Paris, and finally Rapallo, where he had lived for over twenty years. His political fanaticism, his enthusiasm for Mussolini and Fascism, his exaltation of Hitler in the radio broadcasts that he traveled to Rome to record during the war had made him a traitor once the war was over. Avoiding a death sentence, he had been interned in a psychiatric hospital in Washington, DC, and only in the last years of his life had he been released and returned to Italy—first to Alto Adige and then to Venice, where he died and where his lover Olga Rudge had him buried in the cemetery of San Michele.

Morli had read Pound's work, seen films, and looked at photographs of the poet at various points in his life. Pound remained an American from Idaho, a conservative attracted by the avant-garde who had been afraid of the Communists and was obsessively anti-Semitic, because the Jews, in his mind, represented usury, and he hated usury. Many have wondered why Pound ruined his life for a political passion that ended up overwhelming him and causing him to be ostracized.

Morli began to discuss his interest in Pound with Fred, who had known both Pound and Eliot; he asked Fred, "How did you come to meet Pound?"

"I went to see him in Washington at Saint Elizabeths Hospital, where he was institutionalized."

"Do you think he was a great poet?"

"I don't know if I would call *The Cantos* a great work of poetry, because it is discontinuous, but there are certainly beautiful passages. I would say that his translations of Chinese poetry are more interesting. I am thinking, for example, of *Cathay*, a magnificent book published in 1915, an extraordinary and inventive translation based on Ernest Fenollosa's notes that Pound, if I am not mistaken, had come across in 1913."

"What is his language, his English, like?"

"His language is beautiful, simple, direct. Pound had an enormous influence on English and American poetry. It was he who edited the texts in the first edition of *The Waste Land*, by Eliot, who, quoting Dante, dedicated his book to Pound, calling him '*il miglior fabbro.*'"

"How did you manage to meet him? Why did you go to see him in Washington?"

"I was a thirteen-year-old boy in St. Louis when I read an article in the library that contained a famous lyric by Pound, and it was there, in that moment, that I understood that I wanted to be a poet."

"So, what did you do?"

"Years later, when I was studying at Harvard, I wrote him a letter. I knew he was in a psychiatric hospital, and he invited me to go and see him. So, I took the Greyhound and went to see him in Washington."

"He was a Nazi, you are a Jew."

"I don't think he was a Nazi; he was infatuated with Mussolini, who he thought of as the new Jefferson. But you must understand that Pound was an artist, he loved to shock, he loved paradoxes, and he was a little crazy. If there had been a trial, they would have sentenced him to death for treason. But they didn't want to kill a poet, so they interned him without trial. Pound couldn't defend himself. He didn't know how."

"What was he like physically?"

"He was robust, he was sporty, did gymnastics, he was a man of average height, with a nice beard."

"Did you see each other again?"

"No, we wrote each other a few letters. Later I met Eliot in London, who was another very important figure for me."

"They say that Pound apologized to Allen Ginsberg for his anti-Semitism when they first met in Spoleto."

"Yes, I believe so."

"What are you writing?"

"I write every day."

"What's life like in New York?"

"I don't see anyone, I don't go to restaurants, the shops are closed. I work, I go for a walk every now and then."

"It's a real shame we can't see each other."

"Yes. Just think, my daughter lives in Brooklyn and I haven't seen her for over a year."

"Do you think the pandemic will be over by the summer?"

"No, but we'll be able to travel."

Morli asked Luke, "Did you ever meet Pound?"

"No, he was already dead when I went to live in Venice. I met Olga Rudge, his lover, in Siena. I also knew his son Omar well; we were in school together, but he didn't like me."

"What was he like?"

"We'll talk about that when we see each other."

Morli also asked Pietro what he thought of Pound.

"As a poet, I don't know. He helped Eliot."

"Do you think Eliot was a more important poet?"

"I think so. Pound wrote a beautiful book in the '30s, *How to Read*. If you haven't read it, read it now. It explains in a clear and unique way how one should write. But why are you so interested in Pound?"

"I don't know, it's connected to my wanting to understand ... I'll tell you later ... How are you?"

"Worried. I'm in Switzerland and I want to go to Paris to see Ada, but I want to get the vaccine first, and I can't figure out whether they'll give me it or not."

Morli called Luke on the phone to cheer him up, sensing that he was depressed.

"Try writing a story."

"I tried to write a novel years ago, but I can't."

"Try again. Forget all your reasoning, forget who you are and write a simple story."

"I'll have to think about it, but I don't think so."

"Don't think, write."

A few days later, on another phone call, Luke said to him, "You know, I thought of something I could write."

"Don't think, write. I already told you."

"You're right."

"What's your idea?"

"A story that begins with a phone call."

"Write it."

A few days later Luke said to him, "You know, I have to study tennis."

"Why? Do you play tennis?"

"No, but my story is set in a tennis club. Mary played tennis."

"Where's the tennis club?"

"Wimbledon."

"Did your wife play there?"

"Yes."

Morli began to imagine what Mary must have looked like when she was young, in a white tennis outfit: a white short-sleeved Fred Perry top, a white wool skirt, white socks with blue piping, Dunlop tennis shoes; her racket would have been a Dunlop Maxply and the tennis balls white. If Mary played at Wimbledon, the tennis court was grass; if she played in Italy or France, it was clay. Luke's wife had been born in Cairo and learned to play tennis as a child at a cosmopolitan club where Jews were admitted. But these conjectures couldn't give Morli access to Luke's private life; Luke no longer left the house because he had balance problems, and there was a Polish lady who came to clean, wash, iron, and prepare food for him. Luke was a very sweet man and an authoritarian at the same time. Morli had been moved when, one day during one of their phone calls, Luke had asked Morli if he would go and recite the Kaddish at his funeral after he died.

Morli thought everyone has their own individual destiny, linked to the history that surrounds them and how they interpret history. The Jews who had managed to take refuge in England, Switzerland, Palestine, the United States, South America, and other countries had escaped the Holocaust, while millions of Jews had been deported and massacred. Pound knew all this, but he had not changed his mind.

When Morli, after a year of relationships via telephone, went to visit Luke, he discovered that during the pandemic he had let his beard grow: He looked like a rabbi the way they are depicted in old prints. He had aged but only in his movements; otherwise he still had his smile, his curiosity, his eyes that sparkled. At one point, after talking for a while about this and that, Luke asked him, "Are you still interested in Pound?"

"Yes," Morli replied.

"Are you going to write something about him?"

"I don't know. I wonder, on looking at his life, his friendships, his poetry, and his passion for Fascism, whether Pound really was a genius."

"Yes, he was," Luke said without hesitation.

"You told me you never met him."

"No, I knew his lover Olga Rudge in Siena where she worked for the Accademia Chigiana; and she wanted to introduce me to a young friend of hers, a poet, Giulio Cogni. Cogni was a little guy, and I knew he had been a Fascist and had written a book on race. He gave me one of his books on music."

"Was he a friend of Pound's?"

"I don't know. Did you know Cogni?"

"No, I've never heard of him."

In the meantime, a taxi had arrived to pick him up, so they said goodbye.

"I'll be back to see you soon."

"Always a pleasure to see you."

Getting into the taxi, Morli was glad to have seen his friend again. He had aged since before the pandemic, but he had kept his sweet gaze, his smiling eyes. Luke was truly a special person.

Morli decided to go to Venice to revisit the places where Pound had spent his last years. He called a friend of his who ran a hotel and who had given him a good price for a room. That was how he discovered a Venice he had never seen before and that not even Pound had ever seen. An empty Venice, like De Chirico's metaphysical *piazze* and the Grand Canal deserted, not even a gondola, a vaporetto passing only rarely. The shops, bars, restaurants, and almost all the hotels were closed. The waters of the canals had become limpid, the days were clear and the climate mild. In the streets you could hear the voices of Venetians who sallied forth with masks when the lockdown allowed it.

Morli and Aloisia had started out after having had the second vaccination; she had cousins who lived there, and they had gone out of their way to show Morli the places Pound had frequented. Venice had played host to the poet's last silent years. Silent because he had stopped speaking, expressing himself only in monosyllables. The silence added a dose of mystery to that controversial personality. But did the silence express a desire for oblivion or repentance, or was it an arrogant way of hanging on to his ideas and not having to justify himself? That silence fascinated Morli because it did not jibe with Pound's great exuberance, the energy of his youth in London, Paris, and Rapallo. That sporty, fiery, irritating man, always with intense and disgusting opinions, had decided to become an elderly sage, practically mute and with an unkempt white beard, a dark cape, and a wide-brimmed black hat, who walked through the streets of Venice leaning on a stick. Pound had known how to construct a legend for himself as a character that placed him among other vilified artists—artists who, despite their talent and intelligence, had allowed themselves to be unduly carried away by ideologies that would then completely tarnish their lives and the judgment of their works.

The problem arose when, among their works, disgraceful pages began to show through. Morli had no ideology or political affiliation. For him, any political regime that granted freedom was the best.

In Venice, Aloisia tried to understand what was going through Morli's mind; she felt he was interested in the man more than in the poet. Pound was a conservative who loved order, a strong man, and the superiority of certain races or peoples over others. Although his poems had drawn inspiration from classical and ancient models, like a diviner he had sought out new talents and new avant-gardes and had been a formidable agent, entrepreneur, and publisher. Morli was fascinated by the contrast between the ancient and the modern worlds in Pound's life. There was one thing that intrigued him in particular: Throughout history there have always been winners and losers, the good and the bad. Men like Pound or Céline were heroes for some extreme fringes. In other words, there had always been and there would always be a high percentage of racists who despise democracy and consider it a weakness, who will forever be in search of a leader, a guide, a demigod to worship and exalt until, along with him, they fall.

While they were in Venice, Morli said to Aloisia, "I've had an idea. I would like to go back fifty years, to when Pound lived in Venice, and imagine that I had met him. I would like to invent a relationship between him and me."

"What a weird idea!"

"Yes, that's true, but I have to free myself of the obsession."

"Right, but what good does it do you to invent a dialogue, an imaginary meeting with him? I think you're wasting your time. And why give importance to a character like that? If you do, you have to condemn him. He betrayed his country and never repented," said Aloisia.

"I don't know, it's a fantasy and I want to try it. I need it to answer my questions. In the end I'll understand who Pound was, who was the man who, in the last years of his life, chose silence."

What Morli thought was that Pound's silence did not spring from remorse at having made a mistake or from the fear of inspiration deserting him; according to him, Pound's silence was due, rather, to his dismay in the face of the mystery of the human condition. When Pound went to live with Olga in Venice, silence took the place of words. It's likely that he was preparing to die. That he was preparing to leave the tumultuous life he had led.

Perhaps Pound did not ask himself what the meaning of his life was and just lived it like an ordinary person who neither asks himself whether it's worth living nor whether sooner or later he will have to die; and so he wakes up, he slept badly, he does not remember what he dreamed about, he wants to go to the bathroom but doesn't feel like getting up because he senses that the room is cold. He thinks he should take a shower, shave, get dressed. How should he dress? The shirt he would like to wear is dirty or in the laundry. He doesn't know if it's cold or warm outside; it's early October and he has never liked the mid-seasons, uncertain between hot and cold. Never mind the sadness of autumn! After a long summer full of sunshine and very long days, suddenly we are plunged into rain and falling leaves, the days are increasingly short, and the horrible month of November, which he hates, is looming. All this precedes the desire for a coffee. But if he wants coffee he has to go to the kitchen and make it. He wants to smoke a cigarette and read the paper, but he doesn't have much time because he has an appointment, and he hates being late. He is one of those who are always early because they are anxious about not arriving at the airport or the station on time.

Morli, on the other hand, loved the atmosphere of the airport, the temporary situation of the traveller waiting to leave. Leaving was something he did reluctantly, but he left all the time. He had to pack a suitcase, and many times he thought and rethought about what to bring and about what not to forget, but he always ended up forgetting something. It was curious how he could be lazy and in a rush at the same time, caught between one thing to do and another so he didn't have a lot of time in which to get distracted, and he would work in a haphazard manner.

Morli was interested in *his* Pound, a different Pound, imagined by him, a human Pound: fragile, destined to be remembered in a negative way by history and literature. Whatever prestigious prize he had won, and despite having been translated into many languages, opinions about him remained mixed. What was the point of Morli's doing so much research? What was he trying to find out that hadn't already been discovered? He wanted to start writing an invented dialogue with Pound, a long-imaginary interview that had to be as spontaneous as if it had really happened; the reader had to read the interview as if it were true. It was a complicated undertaking, because Pound's unwillingness to talk made it both easier and more difficult at the same time, easier because Pound would be sparing with words, but those words had to be particularly incisive. What did Morli want to get from him? He wanted to let him speak freely so that the truth he wanted to tell about himself would emerge, told by him with his own voice and in his own words, not by a stranger. He wanted to know who Pound was and not what biographers, historians, and journalists had said or written about him.

When someone talks about himself or his memories he often doesn't tell the truth, he invents episodes or thoughts or encounters to make his character more interesting, more intriguing and important. Morli thought that even if the character had invented certain things or omitted others, that was the way he created his image as he wanted it to be seen—the truth he wanted to tell about himself would emerge—and in that sense the story was autobiographical, because it was his life interpreted and told by *him*, with his own voice, in his own words, and not by a stranger.

It was thus that the dialogue with Pound, although imaginary, would become real in the eyes of those who read it. He had to decide where to meet Pound; perhaps the best place was a trattoria near the Zattere near where he had lived with Olga Rudge. Olga wouldn't be with him and Pound, who was very well-mannered, would apologize for being alone. He would wear a checked sports jacket, a shirt with a wide, soft collar, a tie with a loose knot, a V-neck sweater, and a dark cape over it. He had very lively large blue eyes; he was hollow-cheeked and thin, with tapering hands, and he was not very tall. Morli would greet him kindly and, without showing any particular emotion, would ask him what he wanted to drink. Pound would not answer. And so they would sit motionless opposite each other, looking at each other.

At a certain point Morli, unable to remain silent any longer, would have told him, "I asked to meet you because I admire your work, but I know that you don't want to talk anymore, and I must say that your silence intrigues me. In such a noisy world, I wonder what those who keep quiet are thinking. What's more, you stopped writing or publishing. I would like to know if you are satisfied with your work, if your poetic streak has dried up. There are many other things I would like to find out from you. Yes, because many judgments have been made about your work, your ideas, your person, the war period, the hospital, your return to

Italy. I would like to know how you feel about growing old, if you are lacking anything, if you have any regrets."

Soon the waiter would arrive with a bottle of mineral water and pour out a glass for Pound, who would thank him with a look. Morli didn't know what else to say. Pound would sip his glass of water and then get up, smile at Morli, and walk away, leaning on his cane. Morli would remain motionless in the face of this unexpected reaction and the fact that Pound had paid no heed to his words, deeming them inappropriate and trivial. And thus their meeting would take place without words.

A few days later Olga who would seek out Morli again and set up a new meeting in the same place. Pound would show up on time, wearing the same clothes, and would tell him, without hesitation, "I don't play tennis anymore."

"You played a lot of tennis in Rapallo. It's odd to have chosen to live for over twenty years in Rapallo and now in Venice. If I may say so, I find it more original to live in Rapallo than in Venice."

"They are both close to the water."

"True, water is an important element in your life."

"I'd like a whisky, please."

"Waiter, can you bring us two whiskies? Thank you."

"Johnnie Walker Black Label, please."

Pound spoke Italian with a strong English accent. Morli is said to have said, "I wish I could read your books better, but I don't understand poetry well, and I don't know how to judge it." After a long silence he would have felt embarrassed by the banality of what he had said.

When the whiskies arrived, Pound would have drunk his in one gulp, then he'd say, "I hardly ever talk, because I don't play tennis anymore."

"Excuse me, but if you don't play tennis and don't talk, what do you do? Do you read, go to concerts? Do you avoid talking because you feel uncomfortable?"

"No, but I have nothing to say."

"You have been very generous; you have discovered and helped publish writers and poets. Don't you feel the need to discover other talents or to do readings of your poems?"

"I recite them every now and then and I enjoy doing so. My friends are dead, and I don't want to have any more."

"Are you satisfied with what you have written or translated?"

"They've been asking me the same question for more than forty years."

"I wanted to meet you to try to break your silence."

"What's the point? I've said what I had to say."

"It's not that you don't speak because you're ashamed of what you did?"

"No."

"Have you ever tried to apologize for certain exaggerations, for your radio broadcasts during the war?"

"Might I have another whisky?"

"Of course."

"Thank you."

"Can you at least tell me if you're writing something?"

"*Fatti non foste a viver come bruti, ma per seguir virtute e canoscenza.*" This is what Pound would reply, quoting Dante's Ulysses.

Morli would have wondered if Pound's was an answer or a fleeting thought, like a passing cloud.

At that point Morli, who had begun writing his imaginary interview, wondered what was the use. What did he want Pound to say? To confess that he had hidden somewhere a new poem in which he said that things he had preached and believed were wrong? That Mussolini was not a hero but a man who had dragged his people into a disastrous war, making a shameful alliance with Hitler, and so on? Pound would have said that he was aware that he had chosen the losing side, but it was like gambling: the pleasure of playing to the bitter end and then paying the consequences to the full. In any case, better to be remembered as an artist *maudit* than as a non-existent artist. Pound would have confessed his fears, his fears of not being a poet, an artist, a creator on a par with his friends—and so, in order to have a secure identity, a place in history, he had chosen to follow the path that would lead him to be considered for not only his poetry, but also his political choices.

Morli would have liked Pound to tell him that first his imprisonment in Pisa and then the psychiatric hospital where he had spent twelve years had been a necessary price to pay for becoming a cause celebre. Had he not been imprisoned in a cage he would never have written the *Pisan Cantos* and won the Bollingen Prize. In Venice Pound had transformed himself into a grand old man, a prophet, a sort of silent icon. He was like an actor, a man who had understood the world of the image and known how to cultivate his own negative image through and through. He was a genius at personal branding, and his life was an integral part of his work. The work may disappear, but not the legend, and Pound was aware of this. Besides, Morli had not been interested in Pound for his work, but for his life.

People remember legendary figures: Mozart the child prodigy; Lawrence who becomes Lawrence of Arabia; D'Annunzio ladies' man; Dante who spends his life in exile, fleeing from one city to another. Morli was interested in artists for their lives and loves, why they ended up in prison or got drunk or took drugs; their lives were over the top, outside conventions. Gauguin had become Gauguin because he had gone to Polynesia; van Gogh had been in a psychiatric hospital and had cut off his ear.

Pound's silence in Venice did not mean that he had repented or that he had nothing left to say. It was the last chapter of an unbridled narcissism.

Silence was a metaphor for winter. Pound had gone from having dark hair to graying, gray, and then white hair, but the mane was always the same. They were the four seasons of his life, and each had a different rhythm, color, role, and habits. He was a rebel, with a powerful desire to be the center of attention. The decision to go to Venice to die had been, according to Morli, a lapse in style. The choice of Venice was one that too many other equally extraordinary celebrities had made in building their legends.

Had Pound truly loved his wife Dorothy, his mistress Olga, the young Texan Marcella? Morli wondered whether someone who obsessively loved himself like Pound did could truly love another person. His affair with Olga had lasted much of his life, and she had managed to persuade him to come to Venice and also to keep him for herself until his death and then bury him in the foreigners' cemetery and later get buried herself next to him, like Igor and Vera Stravinsky. But what Pound had really felt for Olga, Morli could not know.

In Venice Morli and Aloisia strolled through the deserted city and ate in trattorias. Morli didn't talk much; it was as if he identified with Pound. He wanted to write a novel and call it *Pound*. However, if he was to write it, he had to invent something. But where to start?

He could have begun the novel early one morning, in an ice cream parlour cum bar on the Zattere. Pound is sitting with Olga and they are having breakfast. He has ordered coffee and toast, she a cappuccino and a croissant.

They are old, elegant, silent. At a certain point a photographer approaches and shamelessly takes some photographs. Olga and Ezra do not react; they let him do it. Olga is happy to be photographed with Ezra, her man who after many vicissitudes is now there with her, completely and forever hers.

Olga asks the photographer: "Excuse me, who are you taking these photos for?"

"*Il Gazzettino*, madam. I heard that Mr. Pound had returned to Venice after many years."

"When will they be published?" adds Olga.

"Tomorrow."

"Ah, very good. Could you give us one?"

"Yes, gladly. I'll leave them here at the cash register for you the day after tomorrow."

"What's your name?"

"Paolo."

"Good. Thanks, Paolo. He's a nice young man, don't you think, Ezra?" Pound doesn't reply, and she continues. "What shall we do today? Are you tired, does your leg hurt?" He shakes his head.

"Shall we take the vaporetto and go to Torcello?" He nods.

"I understand that you don't want to talk to other people, but your silence weighs on me after a while. Let's go and take the vaporetto. I'd like to at least understand what you're thinking about."

Pound, in a small voice, says, "This morning, in the bathtub, I was looking at my body. We are a body that lives like a machine that turns on when we wake up and turns off when we sleep and then, definitively, when we die. Who knows what life means? Eating, sleeping, reproducing. Well! I don't talk because it's pointless, and books are pointless. Ever since I was a child I've wondered what life means."

"I understand, I understand. Let's hope Cipriani has castraùre; I haven't eaten them in such a long time. You know I really like their Valpolicella. When I went to Alto Adige I preferred to drink Lagrein, but now here I prefer Valpolicella. I know you don't care about wine, and if anything you prefer to drink whisky. In fact, you need to buy a new bottle because we're almost out. Money goes so fast! Countess Rubini called to tell me there's a fabulous concert on Friday evening at the Fenice. I don't know if you want to come; I'm going for sure. I didn't ask her for the program. She said she wants to host a dinner and invite you because it seems that Indro Montanelli, you know, wants to meet you. He thinks a lot of you. Montale has always had respect for you, too, and considers you a master. Here's the vaporetto! Be careful not to slip. Some English friends are in Venice too, they've bought an apartment. He is a professor of architecture. I met him years ago in Siena, when I worked at the Chigiana. He's Catholic, but I think he's of Jewish origin.

Patience, Ezra, nobody's perfect! Have you taken your blood pressure pills?"

Pound nods, continuing to look at the water, the movement of the boats and the seagulls. "There are so many seagulls in Venice." Unperturbed, Olga continues. "It's a good thing you listen to some of what I say. I wish Mary would come because I can't stand your silence any longer. Let's be honest, apart from when you sing to yourself or play tennis, you've never been light-hearted. And what's more you're vain. I adore your vanity, how you are, how you dress. But I think you give too much importance to your appearance. I say that, but deep down it's not really true. Your elegance is different, special. Your friends weren't elegant. Eliot dressed well, he had a good tailor, but he was too conventional, he looked like a banker. Hemingway was a sportsman and he wore shorts too often, and I can't stand men in shorts. And Joyce? We had a soft spot for him, do you remember? He was so kind, such a sensitive and good person. On another topic, when you were in Washington you didn't think about me; Dorothy was with you. You just need someone to take care of you. You know, I can't fathom how I put up with playing second fiddle for so many years. Now it's too late to make demands. We're nearly done, it's beautiful, the sun is out and, even though we're old, this is one of the most beautiful moments of our lives. I agree with you, we don't know who we are and we're afraid, not of dying, but of living. What do you want to eat today, meat or fish?"

"Liver," Ezra replies.

"Yes, yes; you like liver, but you can't digest onions. I'll have them make it without onions; now they put garlic and onions everywhere. Ever since all those people have been coming from the South... It's incredible how badly people dress. Almost no one wears a tie anymore. Now you and I are two survivors of a world that no longer exists. You're right, there's no need to write, but it's a shame! There would be so many things to say. Think about how many things have happened in our lives, how many happy moments, how many separations. I wonder if you're even a little happy here with me in Venice? You preferred the Rapallo years, when you played tennis and chess and there was Fascism. Who would have ever said, in those years, that it would end so badly? It was the war that ruined everything, that put an end to everything. We didn't need the war! Things were so good before the war! Think about all the years we spent apart! It's a miracle that we found each other again, that we're here. It might never have happened, we could have lost one another, and you—goodness knows what you would have done."

"I'd like to eat liver, but not Venetian style; grilled, very well done. And I would like some Dijon mustard. I don't know if they have spinach, otherwise a
spoonful of puree. Now I would like a whisky."

"I don't know how you can drink whisky in the morning. How did you manage when you were in the hospital? I don't think they gave you whisky there. And before the war you drank very little; you liked white wine."

"You know I don't drink white wine anymore, it makes my stomach acid and gives me a headache."

"Hemingway always drank too much. He killed himself because he was ill, he had overdone it. And yet he was robust. I remember when you were in Paris and you boxed. He was better than you, but not by much. Anyway, let's enjoy this day. I'm sure they'll grill your liver. You're too thin, you should eat some polenta, they make it very nicely. I know you prefer mashed potatoes, but you should try some polenta."

"I'd like a whisky."

"I heard you; we'll ask them right now! You're impatient, when you want something. You're like a child."

Morli wondered where that dialogue, the banal monologue of Olga speaking to Ezra, was going to take him. He had written it remembering that many years before, in a hotel in the Val d'Aosta, he was sitting with a friend in a restaurant and the people at the neighboring table were Samuel Beckett and his wife. It was an unlikely place to meet a writer known for his taciturnity. He was sitting next to his wife and had a bottle of red wine in front of him, while his wife had a bottle of white. Beckett smoked small cigars and his wife Kents. She was talking about a niece who lived in Paris and had a washing machine that was always breaking down so that she had to replace it. Goodness knows how much a new washing machine would cost. While she was talking and Beckett was listening, it wasn't clear from his expression whether he was engaged in the matter or thinking of something else.

Recalling that episode, Morli had put the speech in Olga's mouth, making her talk about something else, but perhaps the mention that she made about how Eliot and Hemingway and Joyce dressed were pointless quotations. The dialogue had to be as banal as possible. The only thing Morli thought interesting about what he had had Pound say in that dialogue with Olga was when he wondered about the nature of human life.

Morli understood that what he had written about Pound didn't work. One couldn't not try to understand what had happened during the war and during his long stay in the hospital. How did he spend his days, first in Rapallo, then in Olga's house on the hill in Sant'Ambrogio? What did he do in Rome during the war when he took the train there from Rapallo to record his radio broadcasts?

And when he was in the hospital in Washington for twelve years, had he read books and done gymnastics and yoga to keep fit? Had he received many visitors? Was his silence in his last years in Venice a consequence of this? Could it be said that Venice was the last docking place after a long shipwreck?

Morli had a creative crisis. Aloisia was right to think that he was wasting his time in pursuit of a story and a character that had been forgotten. But it wasn't like that. Morli unconsciously felt the desire not to justify, but to save Pound. He had become a symbol, a hero for nostalgic neo-Fascists, a sort of banner. Morli instead had focused on Pound's silence because that silence was symbolic.

Morli was not able to give a critical judgment on Pound. What had kept his research alive was deciding whether Pound's political behavior was to be factored into the judgment of his work or not. For this reason Morli had wondered how to interpret Pound's last years in Venice and his decision to remain silent.

Aloisia felt alone and could not feel like a confederate, a participant in Morli's obsession; he meanwhile was neglecting their love. He was completely absorbed in research that would not lead him to discover anything more than what was already known. What's more, Aloisia wondered why he chose to write a novel about it, to attribute importance and dedicate time to a dead poet who had already been talked about so much. With all that was happening in the world, wouldn't it be better to try to look within oneself, or else farther away?

Even Venice, which had been a place full of romantic moments for them, had become for Morli only Pound's city, a place where he could try to tune in to secrets that were not there. He spoke of nothing else, or he otherwise remained silent, and Aloisia had begun to get irritated. She loved Morli deeply, she had great respect for his work, but she couldn't stand being neglected, and so she developed a hostile and competitive attitude toward Pound and never missed an opportunity to belittle him in Morli's eyes. "You can't dedicate a novel to that vain, absurd, and arrogant man," she told him. Or, "You won't be able to turn Pound's life into a novel. There are too many biographies about him!"

When she said things like that, Aloisia felt that Morli was not listening to what she was saying, and she began to feel frustrated, alone. But she understood that Morli would not turn back.

Morli decided to go to Rome and then to Rapallo and asked Aloisia to go with him. But she refused to follow him. Morli only wanted Aloisia to feel involved in his research and did not realize how deeply excluded she felt. He persisted in trying to find a way to write the novel that was festering inside him, but he could not find the right form and voice.

In Rome, and especially in Rapallo, Morli tried to imagine how Pound moved. In Rapallo he had reconstructed his days, talked to the few witnesses still alive, but it wasn't enough. He knew so many details, habits, aspects of Pound's personality, it was as if he had found a perfect character whose life was like a series of chapters in a novel, but it was lacking a plot that would lend form and life to all that information. Morli had not yet found the voice needed for his Pound. If he didn't want to write a biography, he had to find characters, construct a plot.

Morli puzzled over Pound's silence in Venice, and it was intriguing to work out why he had lived for so many years in Rapallo, almost as if he had wanted to protect himself; given that he was so fascinated by Fascism and was a well-known and influential figure in the world of culture, why hadn't he gone to live in Rome, closer to his idol Mussolini? Having chosen to live in Italy, why hadn't he tried since the early years of Fascism to have a more important, more recognizable role for himself? The fact of his being in Rapallo showed that this wasn't what he was looking for.

Another possibility regarding the reasons for his choice of Rapallo, aside from the fact that the climate there was good for his health, might be the other side of the coin of his intellectual arrogance: a sort of shyness, a desire to protect himself from the larger world, from the din of fashion and salons. Rapallo, before and during the war, was a simple, elegant place. For an American man of letters, living there for so many years, far from the traffic of the big cities, had been an unusual and original choice. He lived a secluded life in which he didn't need much money, had few friends, swam, and played tennis.

Morli called Fred as soon as he returned to London. "How are you, how's life in New York?"

"Very quiet. People still go out cautiously. Life isn't like it used to be; I'm almost always at home."

"I wanted to ask you what Pound's daily life was like when you went to visit him at St. Elizabeths."

"It was normal. He wrote, he read, and a lot of people went to visit him."

"Dorothy was with him; did you meet her?"

"Yes, I saw her several times."

"What kind of person was she?"

"She was very kind, nice, a devoted wife."

"Was Pound kind to her?"

"Yes, kind, normal."

"What did you talk about?"

"Various things, his poems. Besides, I don't know if I already told you, but I corrected some things that seemed wrong in his translation of Confucius."

"How did he react?"

"He paid attention to what I was telling him."

"Do you think he was a genius?"

"He was a great innovator. A special, original mind."

"Did he regret his political choices?"

"I don't know, I don't think so, but we never talked about politics. If what you're interested in is understanding Pound better, look up Mary, his daughter, who is still alive."

"Did you meet her?"

"No, I've never seen her, but I know she was very close to her father and worked with him."

During that period Morli learned that a Sicilian friend of his, with whom he had spent a great deal of time in Rome several years earlier, had unexpectedly committed suicide. Together they had talked about literature but never about Pound. The friend, given his political ideas, certainly knew Pound's work and understood him better than others. He could have helped Morli interpret his silence. While Pound had chosen to remain silent in the face of a world that no longer suited him, Morli's friend had instead taken his own life. Pound had not killed himself because, despite his mistakes, he was aware that he had made a legend of his life, while according to Morli his friend had not been able to handle the humiliation of being neither a legend nor a famous person.

Morli remembered that his friend had a gruff and intolerant character. Who knows if Pound would have liked him, if he would have chosen him as an assistant or considered him a friend, if they might have strolled together along the Zattere making abstruse and timeless speeches.

In London, Morli had gone to lunch with Guendalina, a dear friend of his. Guendalina was the niece of a famous pianist. There had never been a love story between them, but there was great trust. They had no scruples about telling each other things, and they loved each other.

Morli told her that, thinking about the nature of genius, he had begun to take an interest in Pound. She interrupted him, "A fascinating, handsome, brilliant man! I love his poems."

"How do you know them?"

"Because we talked about them at home. My grandfather admired Pound for his poems and for his knowledge of avant-garde music."

"And he didn't judge him for his political ideas?"

"He never talked about them. An artist's political ideas are always bizarre, exaggerated. They have little to do with reality."

"Yes, but anti-Semitism and racism are unacceptable!"

"True, but if you go to a museum and look at a masterpiece, you see the masterpiece, you don't ask yourself what political ideas the artist who painted it had or what kind of man he was."

"Yes, but there is such a thing as morals, ethics."

"What about Caravaggio's ethics? And yet ...!"

"Did your grandfather know Pound?"

"Yes, I know that every time he gave a concert at the Fenice, Pound and Olga were there."

"How do you know?"

"Granddad told me, because he was proud to have Pound among his admirers, and he also said that the poet is the supreme artist. The artist of the soul's depths. I remember him saying, 'Few poets are born in every century.'"

"Didn't he judge Pound's life?"

"I don't think so. In life, being a winner or a loser, on the right or wrong side, does not make an artist. Art creates art, and then again art is something else, it has a life of its own. My grandfather had great admiration for poets and considered the *Pisan Cantos* an absolute masterpiece. I know because he always kept a copy with him. Poetry is like music; it is not understood, it is listened to. It must provoke and evoke feelings."

"What you are saying is really moving, you know? I thought that my obsession with Pound made no sense. Aloisia says that it won't get me anywhere, but she's wrong. I want to try to defend poetry, like your grandfather. Not only that, but I was also fascinated by the poet, the man in his contradictions. A blend of presumption and insecurity, he also had the certainty of owning, changing, manipulating, using the English language at will and interspersing it with Chinese, French, Latin, German, or Italian words or phrases."

"Yes, you're right. Pound was a great master, an exceptional linguist. Music, sculpture, words all blend into his writing. Now that you're telling me about it, I envy you. You have chosen an extraordinary character."

"In my opinion, that man's great masterpiece is his long final silence."

"What does 'final silence' mean?"

"I mean he was silent. If I had met him and interviewed him, perhaps he would have told me something, but he would not have revealed his secret to me."

"What secret?"

"The fact that he had the courage to say nothing personal any longer."

"What are you working on right now?"

"I have to think about this story because I feel like I haven't thoroughly analysed some aspects of the poet, and I would like to understand why he devoted so much time to studying and translating Confucius. But I'm trying to know too much and in the end I will know nothing or very little."

"What you have understood, and it seems important to me, is his silence. A silence that is a work of art. Your obsession with Pound's silence is interesting. Maybe it's a metaphor to explain that deep down we know nothing."

"I don't know, but I want to keep going with it."

Pound had always been a fascinating man, and Morli knew that, apart from his wife Dorothy and Olga, he had had various lovers. The last one we know of is Marcella Spann, the Texan secretary he had met while he was in hospital and who, with Dorothy, had followed him for a while to Italy after his discharge. But when Marcella had left him and gone back to America, Pound had been upset, sad, and had fallen ill. This highlighted the fact that Pound lived on love affairs or passions that came into his life by chance and left in the same way.

If Morli wanted to write the novel, it was going to be necessary to find characters and tell the story of Pound's passionate loves, the women who had inspired and loved him. He thought back to his Sicilian friend who had taken his own life. He was a young man from a good family, capricious and absolute in his ways, impatient, spoiled, self-confident. He had been educated in Naples at the Nunziatella military college, had attended the school for officer cadets, and had joined the paratroopers, where he had distinguished himself for his courage and intelligence. He pined for a Southern Italy, a Kingdom of Naples, where Sicilians had a place and a dignity different from that of the postwar republican Italy in which he was born. For this reason, he considered himself a Bourbonist more than a Fascist.

At this point, if he was going to become a character, it was right to give him a name: He would call him Alfio.

After his military service, Alfio had cultivated his passion for cinema and literature and had occupied himself occasionally with the family business. He had become passionate about the Beat Generation. Since boyhood he had learned English well and read Kerouac, who became his hero. He had discovered American poets and had been particularly interested in Ezra Pound, the modernist movement, T.S. Eliot, and others who had emigrated to Europe. So, when he discovered that Pound had returned to live in Italy, he started writing him letters saying that he considered him a hero because he had defended his ideas to the end and suffered humiliating and ferocious punishments for it.

Pound had liked the idea of "ferocious punishment" and had become curious. He wanted to know who this Alfio was who was writing to him from Sicily. And so it was that, when Pound took a trip to Sicily with Marcella Spann and Dorothy, he met up with Alfio in Palermo. From the first meeting Pound liked the fact that this young boy, curly and dark, with dark skin, black eyes, and an aquiline nose, addressed him without the slightest obsequiousness and with a certain arrogance. That arrogance reminded him of his own attitude when he was young, when he judged everything and everyone and had precise opinions: hatreds, loves, certainties. This Sicilian boy had not yet written anything, he was a spoiled daddy's boy, but he liked him. He enjoyed listening to his precise opinions on certain things and appreciated the fact that he had come to meet him and pay homage to him in that brisk way and that he had not asked him for anything, he had only spoken to him about himself. He had been polite and well-mannered with Dorothy and vain and provocative with Marcella Spann. In fact,

Pound got a little irritated, almost jealous, when he realized that Marcella was sensitive to Alfio's bold and virile attitude. And so, for the rest of the time Marcella had remained in Italy, Pound had stopped answering Alfio's letters and, when the boy had written to him saying that he would come to visit him in Rapallo, he had refused.

When Marcella returned to America and Dorothy to London, Pound moved into Olga's house in Venice.

During the film festival he met Alfio by chance at the Lido. They had an aperitif at the Hotel des Bains. Alfio was as arrogant and self-confident as ever and passed judgment on the films, actors, and directors in competition. Pound and Olga listened to those rivers of words with amusement and decided that when the exhibition was over they would all have lunch together. That was how the relationship between Alfio and Pound was rekindled, and Alfio got into the habit of going to visit him every now and then in Venice.

The curious thing was that, while Pound was fascinated by Alfio's snobbish vitality and amused himself by having him tell them about his life and his passionate loves that regularly ended very badly, Olga was irritated by Alfio and considered him a poseur, a talentless social climber. She couldn't stand his cologne or his overly refined way of dressing.

Pound didn't notice the fact that Olga never missed an opportunity to criticize Alfio, because he felt that all her criticisms, her complaints, were inspired by jealousy. However, since he hated conflicts, he met with Alfio several times unbeknownst to Olga in a pizzeria near the Santa Lucia station. The thing that made Olga jealous was that, while Pound almost always kept quiet when he was with her, with Alfio he talked. Alfio urged Pound to write a political pamphlet in which to restate his ideas so that they would remain impressed in the memory of those who thought like him.

Pound let Alfio talk about politics, but he vouchsafed no opinion. He was now far away, detached from the world, and only music and poetry still belonged to him. In fact, they were the only things he spoke about.

"You see, Alfio, you should write poetry instead of dealing with politics. The world has changed now, and everything will become different. Only art, poetry, and music will remain, like the sun and the moon."

"I don't know how to write poetry."

"Then do as I do and translate."

"But I can't write; actually, I don't know how to do anything. I live and enjoy life. I read things that interest me, I travel, I pursue my passions. I come to visit you because I feel you can teach me things. The reason I invited you to write about your political ideas is that I'm sure many still share them."

"I don't want to think about politics anymore. I believed in a certain world, but now the world is different, and I have nothing more to say because I don't understand the world we live in and the one those who will come after us will inhabit. I feel that art, music, and poetry must be preserved because if they are suppressed or forgotten, men will no longer be men. Unfortunately, I am not religious. I do not believe in a specific religion, but I believe in men who live, who seek an answer to the meaning of their life. I am sure that poetry and music express the feelings of human beings. This is the only thing I can still say."

"What you tell me is very beautiful, and you are lucky because you are a poet. But as I said, I am not. I am neither an artist nor a philosopher nor a musician. I am Alfio, an ordinary man who lives in a world he does not like. That's why I see you as a point of reference. I feel privileged because I can talk to you. You see, you have not only always been consistent in your ideas, but you have always been a poet, and I know very well that your poems will remain, albeit with ups and downs, in the history of literature. You wanted to leave a trace of yourself through a work you believed in and that you felt the need to create. I do not feel the need to do anything nor to leave anything. I live life like a journey, like a film. And when I die, if I have no children, I won't leave any trace. I don't believe we come into the world to be useful or useless. We come into the world by chance, by the will of others, and then we are thrown into life, which is a path with many rules that one can follow or not follow, and in any case we are forced to try to defend ourselves in order to survive. Clearly there are heroes, thinkers, revolutionaries and artists who—through their voices, their actions, and their works—rebel against this, but I am not like that. I do not want to do or be something."

"Now, let's not go too far. You came to Venice to visit me, to talk to me, to vent, to express your disquiet, to ask me to get involved politically. So, you do want something."

"Yes, that's true, but in a capricious, unrealistic way. Ultimately, I don't care whether you write or don't write your political theories. I don't care whether you're a great poet. In fact, it matters to me because it satisfies your narcissism. You are a legend. It's always said that Pound has stopped talking. Instead, you're talking to me now, and that doesn't displease you. I'm neither your student nor someone who is asking you for something or wants something from you. You talk to me. And do you know why?"

"No, I don't know, and I don't care. Perhaps I'm intrigued by the fact that you don't want anything from me and that therefore I have nothing to say to you, and I'm pleased that you've understood that nothing that I write or specify with my political ideas matters to you. You see, poetry is written in the present and then stays there forever. I, like you and like others, live in the present and not in the past; we move forward without knowing why. Chance wanted us to meet; chance wanted us to want to see each other; chance wanted Olga to be jealous of my relationship with you, thereby forcing me to have a secret relationship with you, and this makes it more interesting. I know you are a boy, a young man who wants to see me. By chance I also want to see you. Simple, right?"

"Yes, I want to see you because there aren't many like you. It's a pleasure to look at your eyes, your beard, your hands, to listen to your simple way of speaking. And then you have a black hat, a cape, a cane. I haven't defined my way of being. You have to grow old to construct a character that resembles a prophet, but I will never be able to do that because I am lazy, frivolous, susceptible, and too ambitious. I can't reach my ideals of superman; I'm not a genius like you, and therefore I prefer to be a nobody. I'm privileged that you have chosen to talk to me who am a nobody. I'd like to tell you that I have tried several times to read your poems, but I don't understand them; they don't tell me anything. They are too difficult. I don't know if I like poems. I am interested in poets because they call themselves such, because they write verses that people memorize because they capture feelings. But that's not so true either. Poets attract me because they are rebels. Sometimes I wonder, thinking of you, how you managed to stand being in a hospital for so many years."

"I don't know either. Maybe because I lived in the hope of getting out, and then something special happens. You see, a hospital, a hospital room, is a precise, circumscribed place: habits, gestures, repetitive schedules, long silences, short visits under supervision. And in the long run one gets used to the rhythm, the cadence, the tempo of the days and lives in the myth and the hope of leaving the darkness and finding the light again. Leaving the small, circumscribed space of the hospital to find the big world again, the wide open spaces, the walks, the travels, the women, the restaurants, the hotels, the people. But when the desire to find freedom as the only goal—to get out of that prison—becomes reality and one finds out that soon one will be free to return to life, well, this is scary. Yes, it is scary to leave the simple and repetitive safety of a small world where you don't have to do anything, say anything, or worry about anything to face the tempests of your previous life. But too many years have passed, and the so-called true life you knew no longer exists. Many friends are dead. You can no longer express your ideas except in secret, because they no longer correspond to the world you find yourself in. When I left this country, it was the Kingdom of Italy; when I came back, it was the Republic of Italy. So what? you will say. Yes, I admit it; at certain moments, after my return to freedom, I missed the hospital, the simple life, like a life in a box, far from the events of the world. I came to live in Venice to try to protect myself from the world. I have nothing more to say. I want to be silent and find an inner peace. When I walk along the Zattere, when I look at the water, the seagulls, the boats that pass by and I let my thoughts drift I see my life again, my loves, my daughter when she was a little girl. I see the friends of the past; I remember what we said, our laughter, our arguments. I think back to certain tennis matches in Rapallo, why I lost, what I did wrong. And then I think about when I met Olga and when Marcella came into my life."

"I'm sorry I made you jealous of me with Marcella. It was insensitive of me. Unfortunately, it's my vain side, that of a foolish seducer; but believe me, I did not want to humiliate you. I would never have permitted myself. You did well to create a distance. It allowed me to understand that I had done something inappropriate, stupid. You have had infatuations, loves, but I am truly sick in this regard. I have a desperate need to seduce, sometimes even other people's wives, for pure vanity, without a purpose. I would be happy one day to experience a real, great love, but I don't know if I will ever succeed because I don't know how to go deeply into things. I am fated to be a butterfly; I land here and there or nowhere. You, on the other hand, have had true loves and have built an opus, and now you can be silent, contemplate, remember, and dream. Earlier you were talking about your years in the hospital, about the fact that sometimes you miss that small, precise, and orderly life, about your fears of going back to face the world, or a different world; well, it's possible that I can't commit myself to anything I don't want, not only because I don't believe in myself or because my parameters are too ambitious, but because I'm afraid; yes, afraid of being rejected, of not succeeding. I don't trust myself because I lack inner strength. You on the other hand have always had this inner strength."

"You are too focused on yourself. You have to think of others. Your friends, people of your age or your generation. I wouldn't exist, as a writer or as a translator, if I hadn't had certain friends and if I hadn't worked with them. You can't exist alone. You did well to come and visit me, and don't worry about what happened with Marcella. Nothing happened. I was vexed; it's not easy to accept old age. With my friends, when we were young, we believed in the avant-garde, we wanted to change poetry. Poetry for me was a sacred thing that came from afar. I realize that I am telling you confusing things and that you don't want to be a poet. You say that you have no inner strength, but I do not know if that is true. What would you like to do in your life, if you could do everything you wanted?"

"I don't know, believe me. I only know that many things bother me, and I cannot make the past and the present co-exist. When I think about the future I get scared. You see, I come to you precisely because you are old and have manners, an aesthetic sense, an education that I have learned through novels and by observing my grandparents. Unfortunately, you cannot go back, and you cannot stop history."

"Maybe, but art, poetry, and music have always existed, human beings have an intrinsic need of them. You are too young to be afraid. Old people can be afraid of dying. You say you can't write. Try. Maybe you're wrong."

"You don't want to listen to me and I'm sorry, because it's a limitation. I'm neither a genius nor an artist, and so I feel useless, and I chase after the days, the months, the seasons. For me, as I just told you, you have become a reference, a fixed point. You are a person with whom I can talk without feeling judged. If instead I had written some verses or a novel and I had come to submit them to your judgment I would no longer feel free but rather judged. Instead I am here in Venice with you, you who are famous for your poems, for your silence, and you speak to me as I speak to you. When you die, if you die before me, I will be alone. For now, we have not yet talked about intimate things, for example, why have you had a wife and a lover all your life? Why did you choose to come and stay with Olga in Venice? When we met in Palermo you were with Dorothy and Marcella!"

"Sorry to interrupt, but I didn't ask if you play tennis."

Alfio smiled. "Yes, I play tennis."

"Where do you play?"

"Most of the time in Taormina."

"Do you play on clay, grass, or cement?"

"On clay."

"What a shame we didn't meet before, I would have liked to play tennis with you in Taormina. Do you play chess?"

"Not well, but I know how to play."

"Then next time we see each other, if you want, we can play chess."

"Yes, but I'm afraid you'll get bored, because I play too badly."

"I play badly too, but I enjoy it. It is important to have fun! I think I feel good with you, and I talk to you because you don't ask me anything, but you are intelligent, and we can talk about anything. It doesn't matter if you're not a poet or an artist. I think you're becoming my friend."

"Thank you. What you say moves me and fills me with pride. You can't imagine what it means to me to know that I am becoming a friend to you. I'll come visit you soon, we'll find a different place, and maybe we'll take a walk."

"Come whenever you want. Let's try to play chess."

Morli knew that Olga was possessive because living those years in Venice with Pound was her entire life. A life in which she always played second fiddle. Yes, because Dorothy was Pound's wife and had been appointed his guardian when he had left the hospital. Pound could not touch or dispose of money without Dorothy's consent. Ezra could not or would not decide to choose between Dorothy and Olga. In the end, however, when Dorothy had retired to England, Pound began to live with Olga in Venice and travel with her.

Olga had no time to waste because she was no longer young, and Pound was old and unwell, so she had to take advantage of all the time she had with him. Olga had understood that Pound wanted to see Alfio, he no longer needed to have a young woman like Marcella Spann around him. He needed a friend. Olga was sorry to think, however, that Pound always needed someone else. But she had not tried to become friends with Alfio, to make sure that the three of them would be seen together. She couldn't stand being number three any longer, she wanted it to be just her and him.

But things got complicated when Alfio decided to rent an apartment in Venice. It would have been more difficult to see Pound secretly, without Olga knowing. It would have become known that he had moved to Venice. This amused and at the same time disturbed Pound, because it was more difficult for him to find excuses with Olga to be alone. If Olga happened to be away from Venice, she arranged for Mary, their daughter, to come and stay with her father. He had thought of introducing Alfio to Mary, but he didn't do so because if she had been with them he would no longer have felt free to talk to Alfio.

One afternoon he and Alfio had decided to meet in Campo Santo Stefano and go for a walk. Pound had managed to free himself from Olga for a few hours, but shortly after he had met up with Alfio, they ran into her. She was unexpectedly nice to Alfio. "I heard the good news that you have come to stay in Venice!"

"Not really to stay. I'm renting an apartment because I'm working on a project."

"Oh, really?" Olga asked.

"Yes, I'd like to contribute to a RAI documentary about Byron in Venice."

"Wonderful! Walking with an American poet and studying an English poet."

"True."

"Sorry, but I'm busy and I have an appointment. Ezra, see you at home later."

Pound hadn't said anything, but the meeting had put him in a bad mood.

"Don't worry about Olga. We'll find a way to see each other without her knowing," Alfio said. He had immediately noticed his friend's agitation: Pound said, "I don't like this situation, it makes me feel so old. Yes, old, because I'm not free. You see, when I was in prison in Pisa or in the psychiatric hospital in Washington, in a strange way—it may seem like a paradox—I felt free. Yes, because it was my life, my destiny, and now I no longer feel free because I cannot live without Olga. If I must hide, it means that our relationship is false."

"Let's not exaggerate! Olga loves you very much, she takes admirable care of you, but she is suspicious of me. She thinks I am a bad influence on you, that I make you dream and remember other moments of your life in which she was not present. Forgive me if I dare to tell you, but perhaps you don't realize how much you have made Olga suffer for so many years."

"I realize, yes, I realize that I am old, I realize my own deaths, and I will die soon too. I don't know why, but I'm sorry to leave because I don't know where I'm going; probably nowhere, into the dark. Is it true that you're going to make a documentary about Byron?"

"No, it's not true. I'm coming to stay in Venice because you are here and I can watch you walk from afar, I can leave you a letter in a café. No, I won't make a documentary about Byron. I have no talent; I've already told you that. I wouldn't

know where to begin. You don't want to understand because you don't know what it means to have no talent!"

"Forgive me, but I don't feel like talking anymore. I
want to go home, I want to be alone."

"I understand. May I accompany you?"

"No, I just told you, I want to be alone."

That evening Olga asked him: "Do you believe that Alfio is working on a project about Byron?"

"No, I don't believe it."

"Just as well that you're sincere. He came to Venice just to be close to you, there's no doubt about that!"

"It's possible, but ..."

"What hurts me, what irritates me, is that you chose to talk to that boy, to confide in him. But you never talk to me and my friends. I'm sorry that you don't talk to me, I don't know if you realize it or if you notice! It's very offensive."

"It's strange that you should say that to me. You're wrong. I don't want to talk to him or anyone else anymore. It also bothers me that Alfio came to stay in Venice; it bothers me that, as you say, he came for me, to talk to me. It distracted me to see him every now and then, by chance; it was like talking to a priest in the confessional. You talk, the priest listens to you, but he is a stranger. Alfio is a stranger, a person outside my life, but now he has come here and has become intrusive, and I am no longer interested."

"What you say is cruel toward that young man who adores you, admires you, hangs on your every word. And now you can't stand him anymore because he has become a reality, a responsibility. You hate responsibilities. I'm well aware that only Dorothy has been your wife. I never told you, but when you were in the hospital I wrote a letter to Hemingway asking him to help you get out. In reply he said, clearly and sincerely, that he couldn't help you, that your case involved judges, doctors, politics, and he was just your friend. Then he ended the letter by saying that he wanted to tell me, in all sincerity, that he had a lot of sympathy for Dorothy."

"Dear old Hemingway! We were fond of each other, and we liked boxing. I've always been terrible at boxing. At tennis, without boasting, and you know it, I play quite well. Dorothy is cold, but she's beautiful and Hemingway liked her. But I don't think there was anything between them. I'm cold; shall we have tea?"

"You loved Dorothy more than me. After all, you're a bourgeois. You liked Dorothy being your wife, that's all. Now that she's back in England, it's convenient for you to be with me here in Venice, in silence. Then, since it would be ridiculous at this point for you to be infatuated with a girl, you seduced—yes you seduced with your personality—a lost, desperate young man, who found in you a raft, an anchor, and you allowed yourself to go along with that and talked to him about yourself, about your thoughts. And who knows what else! And now you go home and all you can say is make me some tea."

"I don't remember anything I said to Alfio. He said something to me, but I don't know what; I know that it irritated me. I don't like being flattered. I prefer to be loved, but I need to feel free, you know, and the fact that Alfio is in Venice takes away my freedom. He expects to see me, to talk to me, to listen to me, and I don't want to be obligated to do anything. In fact, if by chance he shows up, comes here, or if you bump into him or if he leaves a message for me at the bar, tear up the message; tell him I'm not here, that I'm not well. Do you think we might have tea now?"

"Ezra, you're a monster and I love you, and maybe I love you precisely because you're a monster, a genius, a poet, a handsome man, but above all a monster. Look, you don't have to stay at my place or with me. You can stay with whoever you want, wherever you want. Feel free, but you should start writing again. Write something new, unique, unexpected. Something you never thought of writing before. You haven't written for too long. If you want to dictate instead of writing, and you don't want me to know what you have dictated, let's find a stenographer. I have been in love with you all my life because you were special, a monster, my monster."

"I'm cold, and I would really like a cup of tea."

Alfio stayed in Venice and continued to meet Pound, but less and less often. Olga understood this and stopped worrying about it. Sooner or later, Pound would get tired of talking to Alfio.

"Alfio, we have to stop seeing each other. You must learn to fly with your own wings. You need to find yourself a love, a job. You can't live without working. If you are not an artist, become a farmer or a student, become a doctor or a psychoanalyst. Or, since you are an athlete, open a gym, take up tennis or chess. Try to do something well and give it your all. Life is what it is. I have been wrong many times, I have paid for my mistakes, but I am a poet and I have helped my friends to bring their talent to life. I want nothing else. If they accuse me of being an anti-Semite, a Fascist, it doesn't matter. They were my ideas, and I can't renounce them. My books will live on. If you don't write books, don't worry; it means that it wasn't your destiny. Go back to Sicily. Don't waste time in Venice."

"What you tell me makes sense. I'll try, but I don't believe it. I am Sicilian, I am not American or a Protestant. I don't believe in the work ethic, duties and obligations. You may say to me 'you're spoiled'; perhaps you're right, but I don't care if I'm spoiled, so much the better for me. As you know, I live on a small income and, since I have frugal tastes, I don't need to work. Anyway, thank you, I will follow your advice and return to Sicily. Before I leave, however, I would like to say goodbye to Olga and invite you to lunch at the Cici guesthouse. I want Olga to know that our meetings never took anything away from her. You are a master, and I have come to listen to you and try to learn something."

Pound smiled and asked him, "What have you learned?"

"I have learned to understand what a poet is."

"What is a poet?"

"Someone who lives through poetry. It is his way of expressing his human experience. As you rightly say, the poet leaves his work, and it is up to posterity to judge. You allowed me to spend time with you, to walk together, to be part of your thoughts, your moods. This is an enormous privilege that I will carry within me for all my life. At least I will have been lucky enough to have had a great teacher."

Pound didn't answer, didn't say anything else. Then after a while he added: "I'll ask Olga if she wants to say goodbye to you tomorrow at one o'clock at the Cici guesthouse."

Relieved by the news of Alfio's departure, Olga accepted the invitation and she, Ezra, and Alfio met for lunch. Alfio had ordered a seafood appetizer and a grilled sea bass. Olga was affable with Alfio, and Pound hardly spoke. Olga said to him, "You are Sicilian; I only know Ortigia. How lucky you are to live in such a special place, where the weather is almost always fine!"

"I prefer the North. For my taste there is too much sun in Sicily, and I love the rain. Before returning to Sicily I thought I would go to Austria."

"Does it rain a lot in Austria?" asked Pound.

"I don't know, but I read that Auden loved the rain and that's why he lived in Austria. Auden is one of my favourite poets. We never talked about him."

Pound made no reply, and Olga said, "I detest the rain."

"When you go back to Sicily will you play tennis?" asked Pound.

"I think so. I must also decide whether to get married or not."

Olga, who for obvious reasons didn't like people talking about marriage, asked, "Who are you getting married to?"

"I've known Mariangela, a Sicilian girl, forever. We grew up together. If I am leaving Venice, it's because I need a stable life and I need to take better care of my affairs."

"You are right to stabilize your life, but give us some news! Who knows, maybe Ezra will recover some of his strength and we can come to Sicily in the spring. I would like to go to Catania."

"It's very near my home. I would be happy if you came."

Pound did not speak again. He said nothing about Alfio's marriage, nor about a possible trip to Sicily. Deep down he was happy to be free of Alfio's presence because it had become cumbersome, and at the same time he was sorry that he was leaving because he had got into the habit of walking with him. The truth was that he felt old, sickly, fragile, and Alfio reassured him because he was young, athletic, and muscular, and he liked to lean on him. Olga, who had never been athletic, didn't understand how painful it was to feel less strong, to know that you can't do many things anymore. How much fun it had been for Pound, when he was young in Paris, to box with Hemingway, to go to horse races, to play tennis, to have amorous adventures.

Alfio dropped out of Pound's life; he went to Austria for a while but didn't find the romantic atmosphere he was looking for, so he moved to Milan, where he had friends and where a publisher suggested he write a book called *My Walks with Pound*. Alfio couldn't stand the idea of having obligations. It flattered him that people were asking him to do things, but he knew he wouldn't do them. He could only do what came to mind that day, at that moment. He stayed for some time in Milan. It was an intelligent city, beautiful in its own way; its buildings concealed beautiful secret courtyards, but he didn't think he could live there. The people seemed too busy to him, taken up with practical things, while he needed something else.

He returned to Sicily, not so much to take care of his affairs or to marry Mariangela, but in reality to perfect his tennis. He had it in his head to become a good player, which in a certain sense was a tribute to Pound.

He would never write a book about their meetings; such things were theirs and theirs alone, secret, and he didn't want to share them with anyone. He knew that Pound wouldn't have appreciated him writing them down. Theirs, for a while, had been a special, unique friendship. He knew things that no one would ever know about Pound, and so he would keep them to himself like a precious secret. One of the most vulgar aspects of modern life is always wanting to know everything about everyone. No, he kept the walks and the conversations he'd had with Pound to himself, and there would be no written accounts or photographs.

As soon as he returned to Sicily, Alfio began playing tennis frantically with a coach, then with some good players, morning and afternoon, and soon obtained good results. However, as always happened to him, he was unable to follow through with his plan, and one day he tired of it, didn't go to play, and left by car for Rome. He didn't know why he was going to Rome, a city he didn't particularly like; he went there because he wanted something else. Did he miss Pound? Did he want to go back to Venice? He wasn't sure, he preferred to let the Venice experience remain an exceptional, unique, unrepeatable moment. By now the separation had taken place, it would have been a reheated soup, a melancholic choice.

In the meantime, Pound was bored in Venice; he didn't have his friend nearby to walk with, to joke with, to keep quiet, or talk freely. Instead he was always with Olga, who did not walk and did not play chess, while Alfio played badly like him, because like him he was too fast and impatient. Pound managed to let Alfio know, through a mutual acquaintance, that he was waiting for him in Venice to play chess. Alfio did not reply. He had separated from Pound; something had happened inside him that prevented him from returning. He did not want to be remembered only as Pound's friend. He had learned to play tennis, certainly better than Pound did, and had become a good chess player. These were small personal victories that, however, concerned only him. Pound would never know. Alfio wanted to take his life into his own hands.

Pound had written, "I lost my center fighting the world." Alfio had lost or never found his center precisely because he had always fought the world around him, but not to the end. He was not fearful or superficial. Yes, perhaps superficial, but above all he was lazy and cynical. Only a genius had the sense to get to the bottom of things because his works were destined to remain and change the world. To do things, you had to feel the need for them, and he had felt that need every now and then, but then he had got bored and given up. Since childhood he had suffered from ennui, and even his friendship with Pound was what would have been called a *whim* where he came from. He had managed to get to know him, to seduce him, to become his friend, and to make Olga jealous, but then he had left. He had left forever because he did not want to tie himself down.

He knew very well that his relationship with Pound was unique. And what if his walking away had made the old poet suffer from loneliness? It didn't matter. Like all seducers, he seduced, and then the person he had seduced bored him. He needed something else, anything else that was different and new. He hated memories, nostalgia, regrets. He had never been afraid of losing because he had always left a moment before. He needed the little thrill that the leap into the dark gave him. Not knowing what would happen next, curiosity. But more than curiosity, it was the taste for risk that attracted him, always looking for something else. His political ideals were unrealistic, irrational. Being a Bourbonist, without being noble, was just a thing, just for the sake of it. And Pound had been a gamble, an attempt that had succeeded. Was he bad? Irresponsible? Maybe, but for him the definitions of himself had no importance. Was it pride? Yes, in his own way he was proud of being only Alfio. He entered into the lives of others and gave the impression of being one of them. He knew how to create a dialogue and intimacy, but it was an illusion because then he left. His friendship for Pound, if you could call it that, was an example of this. He had entered the poet's intimacy to the point of being his confidant and then he had left. But what was really interesting about that relationship was that Pound had let himself go and talked to Alfio because he resembled him.

Pound had experienced many different episodes of life and had always left. He had left America to go to Venice and then to London, where he had conquered the English literary scene. After the war he went to Paris and there he had participated in the lives of future great writers, musicians, and artists. He had been accepted, he was an integral part of the cultural and artistic world of Paris in those years, but he had chosen to go to Rapallo, and he had become a Fascist. In Rome he launched himself into radio broadcasts that would lead to his being judged a traitor. He had been in a psychiatric hospital for years and when they had let him out had gone to live in Alto Adige in his daughter's castle, and finally he had returned to Venice, where he would meet Alfio, his last friend.

However, there was a difference between a similarity of character and the reality of the facts. Since Pound was aware of his greatness, he had built a reputation as the great controversial poet *maudit*, and his friends had all become famous. Alfio, on the other hand, was an unknown and had no famous friends. The only one was Pound, but he had distanced himself from him. Because he was not a well-known figure, he did not want to be remembered as Pound's last friend, which gave him a place in the poet's biography and placed him on the same level as the great and the good who Pound had frequented as a young man.

Alfio wanted to be anonymous, to elude definition, because he preferred to be a free man, unlike those who, because they were celebrities, had to live their whole lives that way: They had to be photographed, published, talked about and, in Pound's case, even punished. Pound was condemned to be a celebrity, while Alfio was not. He did not have to account for his choices. Aesthetically he could have a beard or not, long or short hair, dress like a gentleman or in jeans. Alfio's attitude toward Pound might have seemed cruel, but by leaving Venice and not responding to his requests he had defended his way of being—that of not going back. Did this mean that Alfio was an unfeeling sort? Not necessarily. Alfio fled from feelings and had never managed to give a real meaning to his life. He did not want to conform, to accept being a specific thing, for example, a poet or a tennis player, because he knew that not being able to reach excellence, but only being defined as good, would not have had an impact, would not have changed anything, and therefore it wasn't worth it. For this reason he did not go all the way, because he did not want firsthand experience of failing to reach the level he would have liked to reach.

His life was that of a ship without an anchor, without a port. It could not be said that he was unhappy; that's the way he was. He understood that human life, except for a chosen few, was a survival course without a meaning and without a true purpose. He well understood that man is only an animal that is born, lives, and dies and that the meaning of life does not exist. Life takes on a concrete meaning only if one has the will to become a mother or father or if one agrees to do one's best in a job that can be useful to society, such as a doctor or a plumber, an engineer or a farmer. But he didn't want to be useful and so he was a misfit, an outcast. And in truth Pound himself, who after his initial reticence had accepted him and had allowed him to enter his life despite Olga's jealousy, didn't really know who Alfio was. He didn't know and he didn't care to know. Alfio kept him company and that was enough. He amused him, stimulated him, vexed him. But who Alfio was didn't interest him at all. This fascinated Alfio who, in fact, didn't want to know and did not know who he was.

But no one really knows who they are, because very early in life one dons a mask to face others, to face life; and the need to define oneself begins in kindergarten, then at school, then with girls and boys, with work, with family, and so on. You are defined as shy, arrogant, intelligent, top of the class, bottom of the class, average. You give yourself satisfaction and problems, you have quiet or turbulent adolescences, and slowly you form and become something; you put on, as Pirandello says, a mask or a series of masks. Alfio had tried on many different masks and in the end he oscillated between the definition of dandy and intellectual, but none of these definitions responded to who he wanted to be and who he was. He certainly admired heroes and geniuses. He admired dictatorship and did not like democracy because he was convinced that people are not capable of governing themselves without a supreme leader who might be a monarch or a dictator. Since boyhood he had understood that he was neither a genius nor a hero, nor even a seducer. According to him, it was precisely for this reason that he had tried to meet Pound, to become his friend; the poet embodied all the qualities that he admired but did not have.

Pound understood all this well and was flattered: He felt accepted by that young man and in a certain sense he envied him because he did not aspire to become famous. One is famous by destiny or by birth, or patience. You have to accept life as it comes. Pound, who out of insecurity and vanity had always wanted, sought, and ensured he wore one or more masks to achieve fame, found Alfio's light-heartedness attractive. Alfio was capable of living from day to day, without plans, without a goal, without a title or a defined profession nor even a real ideology. Pound, on the other hand, was the architect and victim of his own story. Alfio didn't want a story; he wanted to interpret life as a succession of days, of encounters, of unexpected events, of curiosities, of experiences, because that was the only way he could bear it, going through it like a long divertissement, an adventure. He avoided every annoyance, every obstacle; he accepted losing rather than arguing and moved on to something else. His were not defeats, but passages.

Pound was worried and had spoken to Olga about the danger of a life based on fascination, entertainment, impatience, and superficiality without a handle. His handle had always been literature, poetry, philosophy; therefore, despite his mistakes and the punishments he had suffered, he was safe. Alfio was not safe because he had no handle, and as soon as something concrete and solid appeared that implied the slightest involvement, such as love, friendship, the choice of a job, he got scared and ran away.

After Pound's death, when Alfio had taken his own life, his death was interpreted as a way of putting an end to the awareness of a failure. A life to which he had not been able to give a meaning. Maybe it wasn't like that. The reasons why one decides to kill oneself are infinite, inexplicable, or linked to concrete facts such as emotional pain, a serious illness. But it can be only a fleeting moment, a loss, an unbearable pain. Infinite suppositions can be made, but the real reasons remain unexplained.

Morli was aware that the character of Alfio had served him to begin his novel, and since he had to go to New York with Aloisia, he would try to see Fred. He wanted to know why Fred, after he had gone to Washington to visit Pound in the hospital, had not met the poet again. Fred had replied that there was no precise reason. Morli asked him if he thought he had not seen him again because of his political positions, and Fred had replied, "No, his political ideas have nothing to do with it. Politics have nothing to do with poetry."

Morli was not entirely convinced by what Fred had told him. What he said and his evasion of political events concealed, in his opinion, a certain code of silence. Fred did not want to express a judgement on the man. He had said that he was a poet and that should be enough. There was no point in trying to get him to give a judgment, because he would not have given one.

On arrival in New York, it was snowing, and the city was all white, muffled. The next day, Sunday, was beautiful; the sky was clear, and because of the intense cold the snow had lingered in the gardens, in the parks, and on the roadsides. Morli had bought Aloisia a pink wool beret. The city was still the same, but with less energy, less vitality. Covid had dealt it a tremendous blow. Everyone was wearing masks and walking around with the Green Pass to enter any place. There was fear in New York, insecurity, violence.

On Sunday, Morli had planned to go and visit Antonio, a painter friend who was the son of Sandro, a writer who had been a dear friend of his for many years. Antonio, when he was still a student, had made a portrait of Morli, and now he wanted to make a sketch of him, a charcoal portrait. Antonio's studio was in Dumbo, a section of Brooklyn between the Manhattan Bridge and the Brooklyn Bridge, from where the view of New York, through the pillars that support the bridges, is extraordinary. Aloisia, in Antonio's studio, sat on a small armchair and Antonio made Morli sit on a chair that he had placed on a platform. When he began to draw with charcoal on a sheet of paper supported by an easel, he started to talk about Lucian Freud, saying that in his opinion he was a genius, an artist as extraordinary as Francis Bacon, if not superior. Morli disagreed; he thought Freud was a good painter, but not a genius like Bacon. They talked about American writers who had exiled themselves in

Europe. Antonio asked Morli, "If you had to choose only one writer, who would you choose?"

"Tolstoy," Morli replied without hesitation.

"And among the Americans?"

"James, Fitzgerald, Eliot, Hemingway. I would have liked to meet Hemingway."

At that point Aloisia, who had hardly spoken and was watching Antonio as he went on with his portrait, said to Morli, "Why don't you say something about Ezra Pound?"

"Oh, yes, you're right. I've been interested in Pound for some time."

"Do you know that Dad wrote his thesis on Pound and translated Cantos 91 and 96?"

"No, I didn't know. He never told me about it!"

"Odd," said Aloisia. And Antonio, turning to Morli, "But hold on; you didn't know that Pound was the cause of a disagreement between Dad and Pasolini? They didn't talk for a long time because Pasolini called Pound a Fascist."

"But Pasolini went to Venice to interview Pound for television!" said Morli.

"Yes, of course, but much later. Dad went to see Pound in Rapallo much earlier."

"That's incredible!" said Morli. "He never told me about it."

Aloisia said to Morli, laughing, "If I hadn't mentioned Ezra Pound, you would never have known."

So, that Sunday afternoon not only had Antonio drawn Morli's portrait, but Morli, thanks to Aloisia, had discovered that his friend Sandro had nurtured a passion and devotion for Pound and had been fascinated by his elegance, his presence, his voice.

After that meeting, Morli thought about how unpredictable the parabola of life is. His friendship with Sandro was based above all on their shared passion for literature. It was curious that Sandro in the early fifties, before carrying a Communist Party card, had devoted himself to translating the *Cantos*. This meant that he considered literature and poetry to be above politics.

Back in London once more, Morli picked up his novel again and had reached the point where Pound was feeling nostalgic about Alfio, but Alfio had not returned to Venice and would not even go to Pound's funeral. At that point Morli wondered what would happen to Alfio after Pound's death. But he already knew: He would return to Sicily and take his own life there.

Alfio had disappeared, gone on a long journey, far away, without leaving any addresses. He had decided not to marry Mariangela. They said he had disappeared like Majorana. He had had a mystical crisis and ended up in a monastery, or he had gone to Africa and had hidden or died there. Some claimed to have seen him in Venice and knew for sure that he had gone to the cemetery to pay homage to Pound's grave. But there was no proof. Others said that he had ended up in Brazil and that he had gotten married.

The reality was that Alfio had wanted—and known how —to disappear from everyone, and that disappearance was a gesture almost stronger than Pound's silence. No one knew and would ever know what Alfio had done in the years during which he had disappeared. He managed to leave no trace. But after several years Alfio had returned to Sicily without warning. He had had his house opened and started going again to the family offices that some loyal employees from the time of his father and his uncle had kept open out of respect.

When Alfio showed up, visibly aged, with a beard and long hair, without a tie, in an old jacket and crumpled corduroy trousers, the employees didn't bat an eyelid. He asked how things were going, without explaining or justifying his absence. During those days he had again seen Mariangela, who in the meantime had married a lawyer from Agrigento and had a daughter. Their meeting had been silent at first, then brusque, then sad. Alfio had seen his friends who played chess with him and had gone to play tennis. Everyone who met him was happy to see him and did not ask him questions about his disappearance. He didn't say anything. Everything seemed to have returned to the order of things, as if time had not passed.

One morning Alfio was found dead in his bedroom.

Morli went to lunch with his friend Julian in a small Japanese restaurant near Piccadilly and told him what he had written about Pound and how difficult it was to transform the story of his silence and his last years into a novel. He repeated what had become an obsessive question for him: "Is it possible to judge an artist only by his work, or should he also be judged by his life and his political ideas? According to many, the artist, or rather his work, is above politics."

Julian's face darkened and he replied, "I don't agree. The artist must be judged for his behavior as a whole. Eliot was a well-known anti-Semite, and although he was a great poet I cannot separate his work from his person."

Morli said, "There is no truth; opinions are different. Art is separate from those who produce it. It remains a question without an answer, and everyone has the right to judge as they wish."

"Yes, that's true. But I cannot separate a person from his work."

"I understand what you're saying, but I can't have a definitive opinion. It remains a mystery to me how one can be a poet and a racist. What I fear is that racism is inherent in the nature of certain people, and I fear that it will never be eradicated. Fortunately, there are people like you who do not tolerate any form of racism and who refuse to say that art justifies any behavior. I am trying to write this book without really knowing why. I don't even know if what I have written has any particular meaning. I only wanted to try to portray a man who understood literature and poetry but defended indefensible ideas in his life."

"I understand; but, as I told you, I do not agree. I could never be interested in a person like Eliot, and not even in Pound."

"You can condemn the artist and absolve his art. The work of art lives a life of its own. In the sense that in art and literature only masterpieces survive. But I respect your point of view. I think that a man can have his own ideas about how to lead his own life. He can be bad, choose the wrong ideologies, but if he has a gift, a talent, and the result of his talent is a masterpiece, I think that we should separate the judgment."

"A work of art can be the exaltation of an ideology, but in that case it loses its universal meaning. I think that an artist and his work are the same thing. You instead see the work as something that, once created, has a life of its own and no longer belongs to the person who created it."

Before continuing his book, Morli felt the need to return to Venice and once again visit the places where Pound had lived. He did not want to, and could not, conclude a book by hiding behind a mystery. He had to understand why he had devoted so much time to an American poet he had never met and why, like a diviner, he had tried to find out what his friends thought of him.

Julian's negative and definitive judgment was severe but important. Another friend, however, a famous artist who knew Pound's work well, had expressed a judgment opposite to Julian's. He believed that an artist should be judged only by his work.

Morli felt that in addition to the figure of Alfio, something was missing for the book to become a true novel: What it lacked was a female presence.

Who could be the female character who served as a counterpoint to Alfio? A Venetian woman to whom Pound had dedicated poems, written letters that had remained hidden. She could have had political ideas different from his own, she could have been beautiful, blonde, independent, with a large apartment in a palazzo overlooking the Grand Canal. Pound was jealous of her because she was young, played tennis well, and in the coldest winter months went to the Caribbean to go spearfishing. Pound was afraid that she would fall in love with someone else and that he would no longer have enough charm for her. When she was away, Pound could not stand being in Venice and to avoid sinking into depression he took short trips or returned to Rapallo. The woman was called Vera. While Olga did not suspect anything, Dorothy had come to know that Vera was in her husband's life, and for her it was a sort of revenge on Olga. Vera was flattered to have such an unusual, special, and different suitor from the others.

It was a friend of Vera's who told Morli that he had once asked Vera, "Did Pound talk to you?"

"He spoke little; he mostly read me his verses and sometimes the classics. He had his own age-old and particular way of reading. He had an attractive voice."

"What did you talk about?"

"Sports, my travels, our dreams. We never talked about politics, otherwise we would end up arguing. I couldn't stand the fact that a man like him, with his charm and his intelligence, could have become enamoured of Mussolini. But by then it was all water under the bridge. Our relationship was light-hearted, fun. We laughed together about many things. In some ways, he was childish, naïve, and he enjoyed playing jokes. We invented our own language, a mixture of English, Italian, and Venetian."

"Didn't it bother you that he was an anti-Semite?"

"He was an anti-Semite who had Jewish friends. He said he hated money, but he liked luxury, and he wanted me to tell him the gossip of Venice. He was like that, full of paradoxes and contradictions."

"Did you make love?"

"These are personal things. I can only say that Ezra was a sensual man despite his age. He seemed cold, but he wasn't at all. He wanted to be modern, but he was an old-fashioned man. He treated women with a respect and delicacy that no longer exist today. He was patient with women, while he was certainly not a patient man in general. He liked women and understood them, he knew how to caress them, listen to them, and encourage them. I loved it when he ran his delicate hands through my hair! He said there was something angelic and childish about me and at the same time, when I shook my hair he got excited. Now I wear it shorter; but there was a time when I loosened it and it would fall down my back. I know, I am too vain, but I loved it when Ezra said 'You are beautiful! How beautiful you are, very beautiful.' I saw that he looked at me with real passion, as if he were enchanted by me. He would take my face in his hands and look at me in such an intense and sincere way."

"Did you know Dorothy and Olga?"

"I never saw Dorothy, she lived in England. On the other hand, I saw Olga a few times at the Fenice or at Peggy Guggenheim's house. She was a determined person, very American, strong, possessive, and jealous of Ezra."

"Why do you think he remained a bigamist almost his whole life?"

"I don't think he was merely a bigamist! He respected his wife, and Olga was his lifelong lover. They were the mothers of his children, and he was conservative in his own way and loved his family."

"Did you know Alfio?"

"No, but for a certain period Ezra was obsessed with Alfio. Especially when Alfio left and never came back. He felt betrayed by a friend who had turned his back on him without an explanation. The absurd thing is that he was the one who encouraged him to leave Venice, but then he regretted it. He often happened to make impulsive decisions and then change his mind."

"Olga was jealous of Alfio; were you?"

"Why on earth? They were separate, different things. For me Ezra was special, and I have never been possessive."

"Was he in love with you?"

"I may seem presumptuous, but I think so. I have letters, thoughts, poems, drawings, which were his way of telling me that he loved me. He looked at me with those blue eyes of his in such a sweet, loving way."

"But he was an old man, ill."

"Yes, but when he was with me, he always told me, I was a transfusion of life and lightness for him. He looked at me as if he were an ageless man, and I understood that he was in love with me. He was deeply in love and that was why he was afraid of losing me, that I would not let him come to me anymore, that I would fall in love with a younger man. He wished we had met years earlier, that we could have lived together, traveled. Unfortunately, it wasn't possible, and so we had to settle for brief moments and a temporary happiness."

"How did you manage to see each other without Olga finding out?"

"Olga worked at the conservatory in the morning, and Ezra would come to me for tea. Or he would spend the afternoon, if Olga was out. I think he felt protected when he was with me. Free to say everything that came to mind, without hesitation or guilt."

"Didn't you ever go out?"

"Once I remember that Olga had gone to Siena and we went to lunch at Mazzorbo. He loved Venice, the islands in the lagoon, the beauty. In the end he understood Venetian."

"Will you publish his poems? I mean the ones he wrote for you."

"No, I'll have them cremated with me. They were our things, his and mine."

"Did you hear that Alfio killed himself?"

"Yes, I heard, but as I told you, we never met. Ezra kept certain things, certain people, separate. He liked one-on-one relationships."

"How long did your relationship last?"

"Several years, until the end. Unfortunately, I couldn't accompany him to the cemetery for obvious reasons, but I went to Mass at San Giorgio. He would have been happy to have homage paid to him. He was an extraordinary man. Every now and then, when I'm sad, I go to the cemetery of San Michele and say a prayer at his grave. It gives me a sweet sense of security to think that Ezra is here in Venice forever and that they didn't take him to America. He had chosen Italy as his adoptive country. He was very American and spoke Italian with a strong accent. Venice was the place he loved, the place where he published his first poems and where he chose to end his life. What's more, I am convinced that he died peacefully in this place. Ours was a love that grew deeper and deeper, even though secret. It was something special. When I go to visit him at the cemetery I talk to him, I tell him the gossip. I always have the impression that he is alive and enjoys listening to me. For me, he is alive as long as I am alive. I think about him every day and sometimes I laugh to myself when certain things come to mind..."

"How did you meet?"

"In Venice, at Peggy Guggenheim's house for the vernissage of an exhibition. He looked at me with his intense, irresistible blue eyes. He came up to me and said, 'You are beautiful.' Then he walked away. I had never seen him before, but I immediately understood who he was. Sometime later, at the Gritti Hotel, there was a cocktail party, it must have been during the Biennale, and he was there and asked me for my address. After a few minutes, I slipped a note into his jacket pocket: 'I'll wait for you tomorrow, whenever you want.' He went to the bathroom to read the note and when he came back he whispered to me: 'I'll be coming tomorrow at ten.' I remember that he brushed against me and touched my hair. Back then it was long and blonde."

Morli was satisfied with having imagined the character of Vera. It seemed necessary and romantic to him to add a woman to the poet's life. His last muse. Alfio and Vera made that story more romantic, more distant from reality. He would build the novel only around the last years in Venice. He would recount his obsession with genius, he would talk about Pound with friends and witnesses, he would talk about Dorothy, about Olga, about Pound's real life before getting to Venice and there transforming Pound and the others into romantic characters, keeping only certain things.

But he had to delve deeper into the character of Vera. He had described her too superficially.

Vera had a Jewish father who was a banker in Trieste and an Austrian mother from a noble family related to the Habsburgs.

She had grown up between Vienna, Trieste, and Venice, very beautiful and very spoiled. She had a strong, independent character and as a child she rebelled against the strict education of a German *Fräulein*. Her father felt unconditional love for her and forgave her everything. Her mother, on the other hand, was irritated by her beauty and by the excessive attention her husband had for her daughter. For this reason she scolded her and said unpleasant things to her: She said that she dressed badly, that if she did too much sport her legs would become muscular, that she was overbearing, unfeminine, and that she would never find a husband.

Her mother died when she was seventeen. In the meantime, Vera had become a skiing champion and spent the winter in Cortina. There she had fallen in love with a ski instructor, and they had married, but they had soon separated because despite their physical passion they were too different. Vera had studied dance, had attended the conservatory in Venice, and had always been a great reader. Her father then introduced her to a passion for art and collecting.

At thirty she remarried: an English aristocrat who was a fashion photographer. She had lived for a while in London where she and her husband had had fun, had gone to lots of parties, and taken all kinds of drugs. Her marriage had suffered from the effects of this. It had been an interesting, powerful experience, but slowly, inside her, a feeling of alienation had arisen. She had felt the need to return to live in Venice; her husband had not followed her, and they had separated.

With a childhood friend of hers, a lover of antique furniture from eighteenth-century Venice, she had opened a small antique shop where she amused herself. Her father had left her a lot of money, the apartment on the Grand Canal, and his collection of paintings.

When the cold arrived in winter and there was fog, humidity, and high water, Vera had begun to travel to the Caribbean and had become passionate about spearfishing. She was averse to social life, which she found pointless: boring and gossipy. She did not like romantic intrigues, she had little patience for the banalities of everyday life and, since she had no children, she could not stand conversations in which the qualities of other people's children were praised or belittled.

She adored her dog, a German shepherd, with whom she took long solitary walks in the morning. She had few devoted friends, but most people considered her arrogant, snobbish, and elusive.

As a matter of habit, she almost always spoke in Venetian and could not bear to hear people say, "in Veneto."

Around the age of forty-five, by chance, she had met Pound, and her secret life had begun.

This was in a few strokes the description of Vera's character, which naturally had to be expanded by going deeper into some aspects of her inner life. Many of her defects were forgiven on account of her great beauty. She was generous, eccentric, independent, and secretive.

Almost no one in Venice had suspected that she had any relationship with Pound, and even Olga had never noticed anything.

Pound was rejuvenated, invigorated, and sometimes, as soon as he woke up, he would recite aloud some of his poems or verses by Cavalcanti or Dante. While Olga went to work at the conservatory, he went out almost every morning around ten and, under the pretext of going for a long walk, went to see Vera. She was smiling, affable, but unattainable. She spoke with patience and affection and then grew elusive, answering questions evasively. Her friends had noticed that Vera had changed; her beauty had been replaced by a gravitas and at the same time a different sweetness. It was as if the encounter with Pound had been so strong that it had made her feel something very deep and unique. She felt that she would never experience it again. Her life would be before Pound and after Pound. Pound's serenity had captivated her. Vera had always been restless, too rich, too mercurial, but after meeting Pound something had happened inside her; she had stopped, she had entrusted herself to the poetic love of that old man who needed to love in order to stay alive and inspired and to write poems and love letters. Vera had allowed Pound, because of his love for her, to reclaim his profoundly poetic being. It was as if they had transmitted to each other the *flatus*, the music they needed to rediscover the happiness of being in the world. They realized the privilege of being in Venice, the beauty, how the September light, when the days were clear, was reflected on the water of the canals and the narrow waterways. The charm of hearing few sounds, that of footsteps, of seagulls taking flight, the voices of people talking. Vera and Pound were happy with the privilege of being able to love, wait, and find each other in that unique city. It was important to tell the story of Vera and Ezra's love. This is what Morli had to write if he wanted to give a powerful meaning to his book. Even though he did not respect Pound as a man for his ideas, he had felt the need to add the character of Vera. He did not know if Pound had met Vera when Alfio was still in Venice or after his departure. He still had to decide that. Perhaps it would have been better if he had met her afterward, to separate the two things. Pound would have been nostalgic for his relationship with Alfio, but he would have consoled himself through meeting Vera.

Morli had to extend the conversation he had imagined with Vera's friend, who would have continued to ask her, "You who were a revolutionary as a student and who are a left-wing Jew, what did you find so fascinating in a man who was a Fascist and an anti-Semite?"

"I told you we didn't talk about politics. I don't know, but he was a man unlike everyone else. And we also know that art is above politics, as is love. I think our story was beautiful. As you know, extremes meet. I may seem presumptuous, but I know that Ezra needed me, to see me, to talk to me, to touch me. Ours was a true love story and it remained that way until the end. He gave me a security and an inner strength that no other man had been able to give me until then. I for my part gave him a vital force that provoked his desire, his will to live."

"In what sense?"

"In the very human sense that he desired me, he liked me. He was well aware that he was much older than me and full of ailments, but he wanted to seduce me in every way, and he succeeded. He had something in his look and in his hands that I can't describe, something unique."

"Do you think Alfio was important to him?"

"I think so. He was a friend of his, his last friend, and he was a man who had always attached importance to friendship. When Alfio left Venice he was sorry, but only up to a certain point. I think he also felt relieved. Alfio was a man with some baggage, and that bothered him, that created problems for him, but I can't say anything ... I'm not sure. Ezra would have been very upset if he had known that Alfio had taken his own life, because he loved him. Ezra was a genius, and like all geniuses he was naive, and his political obsessions and his love affairs stemmed from his naivety and his impracticality. He couldn't understand how Alfio felt unresolved. Besides, when he spoke to me about him, he said he was spoiled, lazy. Then sometimes he said he envied him because he played tennis while he couldn't play anymore. He envied me too, because I played tennis as well."

Morli had to invent dialogues between Pound and Vera. For example, she would have said to Pound, "Dictatorships end badly and then deceive people, making them suffer and die. There is something macabre in dictatorships. They often bring out the worst in people and the dictator is like a father, a god, but then disappoints and makes a despicable end."

"But democracy is weak. Dictatorship is important because it represents a mass phenomenon."

"I don't understand how a free and intelligent man like you can think this, how you can be fascinated by the strong man. Dictators are weak, they're liars and think only about their thirst for power by instigating servility, fear, and, even worse, informing on people. What's more, dictators, in the grip of a delirium of omnipotence, always end up making war, and everything winds up in a bloodbath and civil conflict, which is the worst of wars. Do you think I should have ended up in Auschwitz because Jews are greedy and wicked? Can you explain to me why you come here if you are an anti-Semite? I ask myself why I am so crazy and masochistic as to let you do it. I can justify myself by saying that you are a poet, an artist, and you love paradoxical situations, so you do all this only for provocation. I think you are wrong. I don't know if you have had many loves. I think you are too vain to truly love anyone! It is possible that I like you because I am just as vain. What does love mean, anyway?

Poets write sublime poems, and they need muses. But do they really love or is it just a literary fiction?"

"What do you want me to say? That you are right? You know that I am in love because every day, when you are here, I come to visit you and find a thousand excuses just to spend a minute with you and hold your hand. Of course, Dante and Cavalcanti's poems are born from love, and love and poetry mix and merge into one thing which is beauty. When I look at you, I can't believe that you exist, and I feel a desire that resembles an illumination. I look at you and I feel the desire to write a poem. But you want to provoke me, and you do well, because this way I have to force myself to speak and express what I feel."

"I don't write poems, but I know that you have an inner fire, an extraordinary gift, and you communicate it to me. Your words do me good, and I need them. You live with Olga and think of me, you write me notes and poems. I'm not jealous of Olga because I know that you need her to be able to think of me. I'm no longer used to living without you, without knowing that you think of me, that you write to me, that you love me. After the first time you kissed me on the mouth, shyly because you weren't sure how I would react, everything changed. We were together and I knew that we would be together forever."

"What you say to me sends a shiver down my spine, because after that kiss, when I moved away from you, I felt that it was a kiss that would remain inside me, on my lips, and my whole body started to live in a different way. I wish I could write about it, but I don't know if I'll be able to tell how that first kiss felt. The kiss that remained on my lips and in my thoughts for so long. Falling in love is like a miracle, it's like a lightning bolt. You are no longer alone, because another has entered inside you."

"Try to write it down, to make me feel it through your words. Tell me something else."

"May I have a cup of tea?"

"You don't love me today. I can feel it."

"You're wrong. I love you very much."

Vera was preparing the tea; Pound was looking at her in silence.

"Is that okay? Watch out, it's very hot."

"Thank you."

"You're certainly spoiled, very spoiled. You always try to have everything you want."

"I have to go now."

"Aren't you going to drink your tea?"

"It's too hot, and I don't have time anymore. I'll be back tomorrow."

"I don't know why I put up with you. Maybe because you're more selfish than I am."

Morli knew that the pages he had written about Pound were driven by the desire to try to understand the poet's silence and to make him speak, to make the silence speak. He had tried to construct imaginary dialogues, characters, but he would never have a full picture of who that man was.

Morli had tried to write a book starting from a simple question: Was Pound a genius?

Francis Bacon said that he would have liked, as did Eliot, to have a Pound who would say to him "this yes, that no." Joyce's *Ulysses* ends with "yes." Morli's story about Pound could end with "no" or with "May I have a cup of tea?" or with "Can you play tennis?" Or could it end endlessly, in silence; it could end because it could go on forever, but stories are like candles: If you light them, they burn out and then they end. His novel about Pound's silence would end with an imaginary dialogue between Vera and Pound. And then, yes, silence. Only silence.

M orli continued to wonder why he had spent so much time and energy trying to interpret Pound's silence. The silence that was the only poetry he had left. The silence of someone who had talked too much and dangerously, someone who had extolled the virtue of characters who had brought war, hatred, and destruction with them.

In the end, according to Morli, Pound was a character who did not deserve so much attention. The man had been vain, self-centred, absurd and had chosen to be different from his friends, who had loved him and respected him until his choices had become unacceptable. The silence of the last years had not exonerated him.

However, the question of whether the artist and his art are the same thing remained unresolved, without answers. Art lives on its own account. It has no real explanation. You can make many arguments, express criticisms, condemn or applaud. But the work of art is there and lives outside of the person who created it.

Morli knew that Pound had been an artist, a witness of his time, a difficult man, and that history would not forgive him.

After much research, accounts, and attempts to write dialogues, to invent characters, Morli had to decide whether or not he would write the novel. All the elements were there, but Morli had to understand within himself whether it was worth it and whether he was capable of it.

It was the first time that the protagonist of one of his novels was a real person. But what difference is there between a man who really existed and a character in a novel with the same name?

Morli had tried in various ways to make him talk, but he had come to the conclusion that nothing was stronger than that obstinate silence for which he could not give an explanation.

In reality, in the last years of his life in Venice, Pound had expressed himself almost in monosyllables. Instead, in the novel he would have spoken with Olga, with Alfio, and with Vera. Perhaps it would have been better not to write the novel because in no way could Morli respect a man, even if he was an artist, who had been so openly anti-Semitic. It had been a passionate search, studying, constructing, and interpreting Pound's life. It was clear that until he went to live in Rapallo and became enamoured of Mussolini and Fascism, he had been a great man of letters, a formidable talent scout, a friend of writers, poets, artists, and musicians. But this was not enough to justify his frenzied hatred of the Jews.

Aloisia had asked him many times why he found Pound so interesting to the point of wanting to write a novel about him. There are so many negative, perverse, and sick characters in novels; certainly, the controversial, accursed characters have always been more fascinating more than the good and calm ones, but why waste so much time trying to transform such a well-documented real life into a novel?

Unless, Aloisia had suggested, he had decided not to call it *Pound* and had limited himself to taking inspiration from the man—unless he had simplified the course of his life and expanded the characters of Olga, Dorothy, and Vera. And then he would have made a better job of recounting his youth, his happy years in Rapallo, his fury against America, his imprisonment in Pisa, the psychiatric hospital in Washington, and Venice where it was necessary to emphasize the friendship for Alfio and his amorous passion for Vera, describing Olga's jealousy in a more extensive and profound way. But was it worth telling that story without specifying that it was about Pound? He would have had a freer hand, of course, but to what purpose, if that was his obsession?

Morli ended up convincing himself that his long research on Pound had been interesting for several reasons. But he would not write the novel. Deep down he did not want to write it because, even if he had been able to describe that central character with his lights and especially with his shadows, he would have given him an importance that he did not deserve and that he did not want to give him. It was up to the critics, the readers, to decide whether Pound was a great poet, and perhaps he was, but he would not write the novel *Pound's Silence*. He had understood that if that mysterious silence had been given the same importance as a poetic work, then the life and work of a poet would have become osmotic, and therefore if that silence had been presented as if it were Pound's last work of art, it would have been a sort of amnesty toward his previous behavior. Instead, Morli did not want to forgive Pound. It was one thing to study him to understand how to transform him into a character, it was another to breathe life into him and put him on stage.

It seems that Pound had delicate hands and loved to caress cats. But these caresses had not pleased Morli, who was afraid of cats.

Patmos-London, 2023

ABOUT THE AUTHOR

 ALAIN ELKANN is an author, intellectual, and journalist who was born in New York and grew up in Italy. Of international fame, he is the author of more than forty books many of which have been translated into numerous languages, including French, Spanish, Portuguese, Russian, Hebrew, Turkish, Greek, German, Flemish Japanese, and English. His many awards include the following: Premio Cesare Pavese, Premio Internazionale Tarquinia-Cardelli, Premio Capalbo, Premio Letterario Mondello-Città di Palermo, and the Premio Acqui Terme.

Since 1989 Elkann has maintained a weekly interview column for the Italian newspaper *La Stampa*. He has addressed an impressive range of celebrated subjects, including award-winning writers and editors; film stars and directors; fashion designers and businessmen; artists, collectors and museum curators; politicians and diplomats; economists and historians; thinkers and human rights activists. Two collections of his more intriguing interviews have been issued by Bompiani, with whom he has published the majority of his books, while other interviews were collected for the 2017 volume *Alain Elkann: Interviews* published by Assouline, which will release yet another volume of interviews in mid-2024.

His most recent books, both published by Bompiani, include, *Una giornata* (2020), a day in the life of 68-year-old Edmond Bovet-Maurice; and, together with Giuseppe Penone, *474 risposte* (2022), an autobiographic account of Penone's life.

A recurring theme in Elkann's writing is the history of the Jews in Italy, their centrality to Italian history, and the relation between the Jewish faith and other religions. He has lectured on art, Italian literature, and Jewish studies at the Universities of Oxford, Columbia, Jerusalem, Milan's IULM, and the University of Pennsylvania. He has also been a visiting speaker at Cornell University where his work is regularly taught, both in K.E. von Wittelsbach's Italian literature courses and her Jewish Studies courses.

Elkann is a member of the Board of Guarantors of the Italian Academy for Advanced Study in America, at Columbia University. He is also President of The Foundation for Italian Art & Culture (FIAC) in New York.

ABOUT THE TRANSLATOR

ALASTAIR MCEWEN is a literary translator with a career spanning decades. After leaving the teaching profession in 1986, he dedicated himself entirely to translation, collaborating with renowned publishers in Italy, the USA, and the UK.

McEwen has translated works by some of Italy's most celebrated writers, including Umberto Eco, Roberto Calasso, Alessandro Baricco, and Antonio Tabucchi, just to name a few. His expertise extends beyond literature, having contributed translations for the BBC, Miramax–Disney, UNICEF, and the EU. His long-standing work with Umberto Eco included translating the bi-monthly diary piece *La Bustina di Minerva* for the New York Times Syndication Service, a collaboration that went on for twelve years until the author's death

Apart from books, McEwen has translated feature film scripts, opera librettos, and articles across a wide spectrum of industries. He has made television appearances discussing translation and has translated over 120 works of fiction and non-fiction

CROSSINGS

AN INTERSECTION OF CULTURES

Crossings is dedicated to the publication of Italian−language literature and translations from Italian to English.

Rodolfo Di Biasio. *Wayfarers Four*. Translated by Justin Vitello. 1998. ISBN 1-88419-17-9. Vol 1.

Isabella Morra. *Canzoniere: A Bilingual Edition*. Translated by Irene Musillo Mitchell. 1998. ISBN 1-88419-18-6. Vol 2.

Nevio Spadone. *Lus*. Translated by Teresa Picarazzi. 1999. ISBN 1-88419-22-4. Vol 3.

Flavia Pankiewicz. *American Eclipses*. Translated by Peter Carravetta. Introduction by Joseph Tusiani. 1999. ISBN 1-88419-23-2. Vol 4.

Dacia Maraini. *Stowaway on Board*. Translated by Giovanna Bellesia and Victoria Offredi Poletto. 2000. ISBN 1-88419-24-0. Vol 5.

Walter Valeri, editor. *Franca Rame: Woman on Stage*. 2000. ISBN 1-88419-25-9. Vol 6.

Carmine Biagio Iannace. *The Discovery of America*. Translated by William Boelhower. 2000. ISBN 1-88419-26-7. Vol 7.

Romeo Musa da Calice. *Luna sul salice*. Translated by Adelia V. Williams. 2000. ISBN 1-88419-39-9. Vol 8.

Marco Paolini & Gabriele Vacis. *The Story of Vajont*. Translated by Thomas Simpson. 2000. ISBN 1-88419-41-0. Vol 9.

Silvio Ramat. *Sharing A Trip: Selected Poems*. Translated by Emanuel di Pasquale. 2001. ISBN 1-88419-43-7. Vol 10.

Raffaello Baldini. *Page Proof*. Edited by Daniele Benati. Translated by Adria Bernardi. 2001. ISBN 1-88419-47-X. Vol 11.

Maura Del Serra. *Infinite Present*. Translated by Emanuel di Pasquale and Michael Palma. 2002. ISBN 1-88419-52-6. Vol 12.

Dino Campana. *Canti Orfici*. Translated and Notes by Luigi Bonaffini. 2003. ISBN 1-88419-56-9. Vol 13.

Roberto Bertoldo. *The Calvary of the Cranes*. Translated by Emanuel di Pasquale. 2003. ISBN 1-88419-59-3. Vol 14.

Paolo Ruffilli. *Like It or Not*. Translated by Ruth Feldman and James Laughlin. 2007. ISBN 1-88419-75-5. Vol 15.

Giuseppe Bonaviri. *Saracen Tales*. Translated Barbara De Marco. 2006. ISBN 1-88419-76-3. Vol 16.

Leonilde Frieri Ruberto. *Such Is Life*. Translated Laura Ruberto. Introduction by Ilaria Serra. 2010. ISBN 978-1-59954-004-7. Vol 17.

Gina Lagorio. *Tosca the Cat Lady*. Translated by Martha King. 2009. ISBN 978-1-59954-002-3. Vol 18.

Marco Martinelli. *Rumore di acque*. Translated and edited by Thomas Simpson. 2014. ISBN 978-1-59954-066-5. Vol 19.

Emanuele Pettener. *A Season in Florida*. Translated by Thomas De Angelis. 2014. ISBN 978-1-59954-052-2. Vol 20.

Angelo Spina. *Il cucchiaio trafugato*. 2017. ISBN 978-1-59954-112-9. Vol 21.

Michela Zanarella. *Meditations in the Feminine*. Translated by Leanne Hoppe. 2017. ISBN 978-1-59954-110-5. Vol 22.

Francesco "Kento" Carlo. *Resistenza Rap*. Translated by Emma Gainsforth and Siân Gibby. 2017. ISBN 978-1-59954-112-9. Vol 23.

Kossi Komla-Ebri. *EMBAR-RACE-MENTS*. Translated by Marie Orton. 2019. ISBN 978-1-59954-124-2. Vol 24.

Angelo Spina. *Immagina la prossima mossa*. 2019. ISBN 978-1-59954-153-2. Vol 25.

Luigi Lo Cascio. *Othello*. Translated by Gloria Pastorino. 2020. ISBN 978-1-59954-158-7. Vol 26.

Sante Candeloro. *Puzzle*. Translated by Fred L. Gardaphe. 2020. ISBN 978-1-59954-165-5. Vol 27.

Amerigo Ruggiero. *Italians in America*. Translated by Mark Pietralunga. 2020. ISBN 978-1-59954-169-3. Vol 28.

Giuseppe Prezzolini. *The Transplants*. Translated by Fabio Girelli Carasi. 2021. ISBN 978-1-59954-137-2. Vol 29.

Silvana La Spina. *Penelope*. Translated by Anna Chiafele and Lisa Pike. 2021. ISBN 978-1-59954-172-3. Vol 30.

Marino Magliani. *A Window to Zeewijk*. Translated by Zachary Scalzo. 2021. ISBN 978-1-59954-178-5. Vol 31.

Alain Elkann. *Anita*. Translated by K.E. Bättig von Wittelsbach. 2021. ISBN 978-1-59954-170-9. Vol 32.

Luigi Fontanella. *The God of New York*. Translated by Siân Gibby. 2022. ISBN 978-1-59954-177-8. Vol 33.

Kossi A. Komla-Ebri. *Home*. Translated by Marie Orton. 2022. ISBN 978-1-59954-190-7. Vol 34.

Leopold Berman. *The Story of a Jewish Boy*. Translated by Giuliana Carugati. 2022. ISBN 978-1-59954-192-1. Vol 35.

Alain Elkann. *Nonna Carla*. Translated by K.E. Bättig von Wittelsbach. 2023. ISBN 978-1-59954-201-0. Vol 36.

Luigi Pirandello. *L'uomo, la bestia, e la virtù*. Translation by Alice Rohe. Edited with an Introduction by Giuseppe Bolognese. 2024. ISBN 978-1-59954-205-8. Vol 37.

Maria Teresa Cometto. *Emma and the Angel of Central Park*. 2023. ISBN 978-1-59954-157-0. Vol 38.

Alain Elkann. *A Single Day*. Translated by K.E. Bättig von Wittelsbach. 2024. ISBN 978-1-59954-211-9. Vol 39.

Elisabetta Rasy. The Indiscreet. Translated by Siân Gibby. 2024. ISBN 978-1-59954-212-6. Vol. 40.

Joseph Bathanti. *Sempre Fedele*. Translated by Maria Morbiducci and Darcy Di Mona 2024. ISBN 978-1-59954-224-9. Vol. 41.

Sofia Pirandello. *Animals*. 2024. ISBN 978-1-59954-225-6. Vol. 42.

Emanuele Pettener. *It's Saturday You Left Me and I'm So Beautiful*. 2025. Translated by Giorgio Tarchini. ISBN 978-1-59954-234-8. Vol 43.

Salvatore Mugno. *Livery Stable Blues*. 2025. Translated by Carlo Massimo. ISBN 978-1-59954-235-5. Vol 44.